Feb

For the Cades —

a Merry (late) Christmas!

Love,
Tick

DON'T DIE MR. OPAL.

Oklahoma Needs You.

A Group Novel

Copyright © 2006 by the St. Charles Writers Group

All rights reserved. No part of this book shall be reproduced or transmitted in any form or by any means, electronic, mechanical, magnetic, photographic including photocopying, recording or by any information storage and retrieval system, without prior written permission of the publisher. No patent liability is assumed with respect to the use of the information contained herein. Although every precaution has been taken in the preparation of this book, the publisher and author assume no responsibility for errors or omissions. Neither is any liability assumed for damages resulting from the use of the information contained herein.

This is a work of fiction. Names, characters, places, and incidents either are the product of the author's imagination or are used fictitiously. Any resemblance to actual events or locales or persons, living or dead, is entirely coincidental.

ISBN 0-7414-2946-2

Published by:

INFINITY
PUBLISHING.COM

1094 New DeHaven Street, Suite 100
West Conshohocken, PA 19428-2713
Info@buybooksontheweb.com
www.buybooksontheweb.com
Toll-free (877) BUY BOOK
Local Phone (610) 941-9999
Fax (610) 941-9959

Printed in the United States of America
Printed on Recycled Paper
Published January 2006

Introduction

It is in the heart that the values lie.
—Mark Twain, *Eve's Diary*, 1905

This book, which began as a writing project in the minds of the St. Charles Writers Group, finished as a journey of heart. From its conception on a spring morning in a library basement in 2000, through the writing process and three rounds of editing completed in 2005, *Don't Die Mr. Opal. Oklahoma Needs You*, transformed a title and story idea, and encompassed the efforts of eighteen writers, seven of them, dedicated editors, into the book you see today.

If heads alone prevailed, no writer of right mind would have agreed to author a book with seventeen others. That is where heart comes in. The faith and belief held by these writers withstood the logic of naysayers who cried, "It can't be done, it won't be good, it'll never sell." This acquiescence to heart enabled the writers to complete the task before them.

To the writers, the values of this book lie in the act of storytelling, the strength of the written word, and the camaraderie of fellowship, the last, a by-product of time spent together creating, sharing, laughing. We sincerely hope you, the reader, share a sense of these values as you delve into the world of Opal and Jim and Alice and their companions in print.

	PROLOGUE		1
1	LEGACY	Dean Pannell	3
2	TYGER, TYGER	Rick Holinger	8
3	TAKE OFF	Adrienne Lee	15
4	AT O'HARE	Susan Kraykowski	21
5	THE WATCHER	Kim Dechert	29
6	THE BUFFALO CAVE	Kitty Jarman	35
7	THE STARS THROW DOWN THEIR SPEARS	Kevin Burris	43
8	CONNECTIONS	Mike Balcom-Vetillo	48
9	PAPER AIRPLANES	Todd Possehl	52
10	CROSSING PATHS	Maryann Durland	56
11	TAKING CARE OF BUSINESS	Laurie Bohlke	62
12	CHOICES	Joselle Kehoe	67
13	LET THE CARD FALL WHERE IT MAY	Bonnie Harm-Pechous	71
14	HEAVEN'S ROCK	Paul Cook	76
15	DETOURS	Fran Fredricks	84
16	IN FLIGHT	Joe Hebert	91
17	BY THE TIME I GET TO TULSA	Nancy Wedemeyer	96
18	A LITTLE GRILLED CHEESE IS A DANGEROUS THING	Elliott Sturm	103
19	CLOSE QUARTERS	Mike Balcom-Vetillo	107
20	GUNSHOTS AND WHISPERS	Nancy Wedemeyer	115
	EPILOGUE		121

Prologue

United States Department of Justice
Federal Bureau of Investigation

<u>MEMORANDUM</u>

DATE: 8-3-94
PRECEDENCE: Immediate

FROM: Director, FBIHQ FAA Washington HQ/FAA
TO: Agent Jewel, Chicago Field
CLASSIFICATION: Secret — Eyes Only

Re: In-flight explosion/crash of Dash 8 Flight 3355, July 30, 1994

Jewel:

Gather all video tape regarding crash site rescue effort made by television media and local law enforcement.

Scrutinize all persons at the scene including rescue teams, victims and bystanders. Examine and report.

Passenger Manifest enclosed. Check insurers and victims' wills per normal procedure.

You will be promptly informed as new matters come to our attention.

Sincerely,

K.T. Jennings
Director

Chapter One
LEGACY
Dean Pannell

Dan is cold, wet and deathly afraid. The warm flow of blood on his cheek is overwhelmed by the cold rush of water at his feet. His suit is ruined; the client will be furious; and the Lake Michigan water won't stop rushing into the brutally torn Dash 8. He had never liked flying on the little turbo props, but he'd never make a living without them, so he put up with the discomfort. It was a very handsome living, a point of no little pride when he went back home for holidays.

His right arm is completely numb, but Dan is sure that it's still there. His right leg hurts, overwhelming a thousand little hurts that he would not notice until later. Fighting the fear of what he will see, Dan turns his head and looks down. The arm is bloody and mangled, but still attached. Slowly his gaze shifts up and over to the man in the window seat. Horror grabs his throat and he cannot scream. The man is sitting there, blissfully unaware. His head is not.

The red-black fog of unconsciousness creeps in from the edges of nowhere and Dan's breath comes quick and shallow. Before the black noose completes its embrace, he can feel a hand gently but firmly testing his right arm and leg. Dan manages somehow to look up into Charles Castro's face, watching him as he struggles to unfasten Dan's seatbelt. Recognition gives way to fleeting panic. Castro was the flight attendant, and Dan had been joking loudly with the man in the window seat, laying odds on Castro's sexual preferences. Dan knew he'd been heard, but didn't care—until now. He looks up to see Charles Castro working inside that fragile little airplane, wet, cold and in deadly danger. His straining face is red and distorted from the effort of moving Dan's useless body. Each movement brings pain. Dan surrenders to the crushing blackness. The face of this unlikely angel is the last thing he sees.

Massachusetts, 1996

The day had started well.

He had risen at four a.m. by instinct, no longer needing an alarm.

Daniel O'Keefe had grown up on the water, the son of a fisherman father, fisherman grandfather, great grandfather and uncountable generations back before the time when children became accountants and senior strategic analysts; a true son of Gloucester Harbor. The Portuguese in him, his grandmother's legacy, had plowed the salt spray before Columbus, and had seen all the world when the world was all there was to see. And now he rose at four every morning. A disease of the blood, perhaps.

Dan stumbled into the bathroom, scratching his curly black hair and squinting at the bright fluorescent light. He slept nude, but didn't glance at his lean, muscular frame in the mirror as he hurriedly pulled on jeans and a gray turtleneck followed by a grease-stained navy parka. He could almost smell his first cup of coffee as he stepped out the front door.

The morning was February crisp, but not biting. The smell and taste of salt air mixed nicely with the stout wake-me-up coffee from Rosie's pot. The Good News Diner served no espresso drinks and likely never would. Like most midwinter mornings, he went to work at his Uncle Roger's garage. Dan could fix nearly anything, and nearly anything was likely to come through the old twelve-foot wooden garage doors. He didn't take his boat out on winter waters though he could easily sign aboard a tuna boat. Instead, he revived engines at Roger's shop. He also did the books; one lonely vestige of a life that had ended two years before.

This morning, a customer brought in an old Studebaker Hawk for Dan to look over. It had the super-charged engine - hell to work on and nearly impossible to find parts for, but it was wonderful to hear and Dan loved to make it run just right so he could listen to that perfect old sound.

The day had started well indeed.

Now, with the day's work done and safe in the embrace of his home, Dan was that good tired you get from a day of doing something hard that you love. No matter that every bone ached and every muscle cried; the soul was satisfied. He thought nothing of the flashing light on his answering machine. Dan had many friends and the light was always flashing. Business as usual.

And then he heard her voice.

"Dan?"

It was Alice.

"Dan?" she said again, clearing her throat. "Charles is dying. Please call me as soon as you can. There's not much time."

Dan played the message again. They'd kept in touch, he, Alice, Jim and Charles. Airplane crash survivors did that, he guessed. In fact, only two survivors ever flew again—Alice, of course, a pilot who flew home to Oklahoma; and Rod O'Neal, another passenger on that flight, who was shuttling between venture capitalists looking for someone to invest in his company. A slick businessman, he seemed to be the only one unaffected by the crash.

The others stayed firmly on the ground. Jim went back to Tennessee alone. His wife, Juliana, and his parents had been claimed by the crash and the black waters of Lake Michigan. Charles had moved west and opened a coffee shop in San Luis Obispo, south of San Francisco. Dan left Chicago as far behind him as he could and returned to Massachusetts, to the family home in Gloucester. He left everything he owned for the landlord to sell. Didn't want it. Didn't want to see it. Didn't want to touch it. He left accounting behind as well. After the accident, he never looked at another ledger until the day he dumped Roger's shoebox of receipts on the old garage desk and straightened out the accounts. Roger was the best mechanic around. With Dan's help, he became the most profitable.

Dan knew what he had to do. Charles had saved his life. He would go to California. He had to say thank you one more time. Charles would understand if he didn't come, but Dan would never forgive himself. He reached for his small black address book and found Alice's number. He dialed the phone and his mind wandered as he waited for Alice to answer.

The flashing lights jar Dan awake. The choppy roar of the Med Evac copter rushes off in a vain attempt to save some poor soul who won't last the night.

Dan is strapped into a stretcher out on the tarmac and immobilized from head to toe. He can barely move his eyes, let alone anything else. Half a dozen ambulances are lined up impatiently waiting for their cargo as paramedics and doctors work feverishly to save those who lie too close to the edge of life. Television crews have arrived, their cameras and microphones competing with the victims for attention. Sirens cut through the clamor as the first ambulance leaves for the hospital. Dan feels relieved, for once, being ignored. His injuries must not be life threatening.

Dan finds just enough wiggle in the head restraint to scan the growing crowd with his peripheral vision. Rubbernecking ambulance chasers try to figure out who's already dead and who will be dead soon. Some faces wear the worry of family and friends. One face is different. It carefully scans the survivors on the tarmac. It passes by Dan briefly and leaves him cold to the bone, though he can't make out its features. Walking from victim to victim, it studies survivors until it's standing before Jim's stretcher. It hesitates and takes a step closer, then disappears as paramedics approach.

"Hello?" Alice answered on the fourth ring. Dan jumped.
"Alice? It's Dan. I got your call. What's going on?"
"Oh Dan, Charles's dying. He only has a few weeks."
"Has anyone told Jim?"
"I talked to him a little while ago, and I left a message for Rod. Jim wants to go see Charles. Says he can meet me in Chicago. He's taking the train up from Nashville the day after tomorrow. I'll be flying in from Oklahoma that night. We're trying to figure out what to do from there. Jim's still not flying, you know."

"I'm not flying yet, either," said Dan, a prickle of fear scratched between his shoulder blades. "Listen, I'll give Jim a call and tell him I'll pick him up at the station and we'll meet you at O'Hare. We can drive out to see Charles in my car."

"You sure, Dan?"

"Yeah, how else will Jim and I get there?" Dan laughed nervously.
"Okay... Dan?"
"Yeah?"
"Thanks."
"You got it. I'll see you soon."
Dan put down the telephone. He stood for a moment, silently studying the living room walls that had embraced so many generations. He picked up the phone to call his uncle to let him know he was heading west to see his friends.

Chapter Two

TYGER, TYGER

Rick Holinger

Nashville

From upstairs came the sound of a fight, the wife-beater throwing punches. Jim heard a scream then the thud when she landed. He grabbed the broom and rapped the handle hard on the ceiling.

The husband swore at him.

"Anytime, man, anytime," Jim whispered back.

But he knew the fat pig would never try anything. Even though the guy was almost thirty years younger and boxed in a gym, the dude was scared of Jim. He'd probably seen *Rambo* too many times, and was afraid Jim was one of those killing machines that couldn't be turned off when they left the jungle. Probably been around the night that Jim had shot put the guy he caught banging his wife out the screen door, right through the only renovated part of the apartment. He was still paying for that.

Jim took the coffeepot off the hotplate and poured a steaming mug of light-brown water and black grounds into the Mickey Mouse cup that he'd light-fingered at a sidewalk sale. He picked up the Blake and unwound the rubber bands holding it together. God, he could hardly read it; the pages were smeared with dirt and newsprint. It's all here, he thought: life, death, and everything in-between.

> *Tyger, Tyger, burning bright,*
> *In the forests of the night;*
> *What immortal hand or eye,*
> *Could frame thy fearful symmetry?*

From the apartment next to his, where the gay history student lived, came the methodical digital pounding bass of Eiffel 65. He knew the name because the time he pounded on the dude's door and yelled, "What's that god-awful crap you're playing?" The boy thought he was taking an interest in the music and told him. The kid was okay. Jim, at his age, played The Doors and The Rolling Stones just as loudly, probably louder. Joplin. Hendrix. Musicians, composers, saints.

*And what shoulder, & what art,
Could twist the sinews of thy heart?*

You gotta live life to love it. Napalm hadn't burned that dictum out of him. He grabbed an Oreo from the open package, scaring a roach out from underneath. He let it go.

'Nam had helped him more than hurt him. Hardened him to how things were: random and chaotic, without form. Cast him from the innocence of childhood, even with his college education, into the experience of adulthood. Camus, Sartre—they knew the Essence of life came in Existence, the experienced life, not thought-about life. Live in the extreme; feel passionately; see the world in a grain of sand and heaven in a wildflower.

Juliana thought differently. She thought he needed her because she needed him. Maybe he had before Southeast Asia, before the heat, the drugs, the claymores. She'd been taken as much with his money as with him. Or rather his parents' money—the house in Winnetka, the cabin in Wisconsin, the condo in Vail, the yacht moored in the Keys. She thought his Existential talk was his way of impressing her, and she read just enough to keep up with him. He had gotten married to please her, his parents, her parents, their friends. Society at large. And it hadn't hurt that she was a knockout, with long, curly auburn hair.

When he got out of the Army—decorated, intact— Juliana thought they could make it. But time and separation wore her down. Even after he dragged her to Nashville because he loved the irony of a Blakean Existentialist living in Elvis's backyard, she pleaded with him to take a vacation, get out of their *squalid*—her word—one-room apartment.

Somewhere idyllic. Door County, Wisconsin, would work. Get away from Nashville's honky-tonk, its aging hookers.

"Forgive and forget," she'd said about her one-night stand. "You've been through hell, and I'm your angel who's going to pick up your pieces and put you back together, just like we replaced that screen door. Better than new. This trip will save you. Save us."

A flash. A light brighter than any sun he'd ever seen in 'Nam or the Tennessee tenements. Paradise Lost. Zoom, right into Lake Michigan.

Why hadn't he mentioned the flash to the investigators when they sat him down? Because he knew they distrusted him already, a big six-foot, three-incher bearing an unkempt beard and a camouflage get-up. Because they had already sized him up as crazy, so why encourage the obvious?

What the hammer? What the chain,
In what furnace was thy brain?

The first time he'd seen the De Havilland Dash 8, he saw a coffin with wings. He had to give it to the pilot, turning his Airbus into a boat, using the waves to slow them, each humpbacked crest banging into them like cannon fire, the fuselage holding together, but some passengers dead by the time it stopped. One man bashed in the head from flying debris; a child not tucked in tight catapulted into the cabin's forward wall.

When the stars threw down their spears
And water'd heaven with their tears:
Did he smile his work to see?
Did he who made the Lamb make thee?

He never saw Juliana again.

When the telephone in the hall rang. Jim heard the history student open his door. "Hello? Yeah, sure, hold on." A pause. "Jim? You home?"

Chicago

The train squealed into the station a number of hours late. Jim had lost count. Frozen switches, the conductor said. Waiting on the fringe of Chicago's Loop, he'd given up reading Blake and begun drinking the miniature Johnnie Walker Red bottles available in the club bar.

The skyline hadn't changed since he'd been here last. It looked like his freezer did before he defrosted it every few months, a conglomeration of huge frozen statues. The snow and sub-zero temperatures were making national news on the laptop of the young guy who sat beside him.

"Where you headed once we get in?" the kid had asked. "Maybe we could split a cab."

"Someone's picking me up," Jim smiled. "Sorry."

He could have offered this young exec a ride, offered Dan's Buick. But no, not this one. He had his computer to help him. Those dot-com pissants tell people that's all they need to live, so let's see him hail a taxi with it.

When the train finally stopped in the station, Jim waited for the herd of mommas, poppas, and children, the grandparents and college kids to pull their wheeled luggage off the overheads and down the aisle, pull on padded coats, parade out the door and down the platform. When the car had emptied, he unsheathed his JCPenney's shopping bag from under the seat and threw his green khaki army coat around his shoulders. Silver cars hissed beside him. Locomotives bled blue smoke.

The diesel exhaust reminded him of the luxury trains he rode in with his mother and father, sleeping in a giant rolling bedroom fit for the three of them when vacationing to Florida, California, New York. They'd eaten in dining cars with fine linen, place settings, service and food better than most four-star restaurants. He remembered how his parents told him to always treat the colored porters nicely. "After all, they're people, too, just like us. But not really, dear." Because when Martin Luther King, Jr. came to Chicago, his mother told him the man was coming to stir up trouble, and his father at dinner complained about the lazy coloreds who worked at the hospital, nurses who never got anything right and janitors who were always late.

In high school he had figured out how hypocritical and racist his parents were. Then, in college, his religion teacher pointed out the difference between World War II and the conflict in Vietnam: one a war to contain a demonic tyrant, the other a civil war to reunite a split country. It enlightened Jim to the fact that his parents were blindly patriotic in supporting the war, but did not keep him from volunteering for duty. Because why go through life wearing blinders of tradition and routine? Why not feel the extremes life offered like gifts? If his parents wanted to live the WASP dream of earning a lot of money, going to church and sending their children to the right camps and schools, fine for them. They had fulfilled their dream. But not his. All that money and what did it get them? A watery grave.

Jim had rejected every penny of his parents' millions—left it to the suits to handle. Now, poor as he chose to be, as little as he owned, Jim was leading a better life than the robots around him. He was conscious of every second in every hour in every day. Everyone else either fretted about the future or sentimentalized the past. For him only the Now mattered.

But when the call came from Alice, he knew he must give up the present, at least for the time it took to go into the past, to go west.

Jim's first memory in the hospital was a doctor telling him that only five people had survived the crash. "Juliana? My parents?"

The doctor shook his head, "Jim, I'm sorry."

The next day he met Alice, another survivor. She explained how Charles had lifted Jim's limp body and pushed it through the ripped fuselage. He handed Jim over to those already aboard the inflated raft before diving back for another try at survivors.

Through the station's automatic doors, the steamy heat pressing in on him, he spotted Dan; his bright yellow slicker sticking out from commuter gray, brown, and blue. He looked lost.

"Dan. It's Jim."

Dan swung to face him, a broad grin lighting his face, a hand out to greet him.

"Jim. I was looking ... I hate crowds."

Jim studied the hand waiting to be shaken and decided to ignore it, instead surrounding the yellow slicker with both arms in a bear hug. He pressed his head against Dan's. Alice had told Jim that Dan had taken up commercial fishing, and he felt the fisherman's strong arms squeeze back. Jim watched the crush of commuters take in the two men, then hurriedly looked away. The flat gray-blue neon lights, the wool caps and the pink faces began to blur. He blinked back the tears once, then let them go.

Dan broke away first. "We've got to pick up Alice," he said, avoiding Jim's eyes. "She's flying in. She wanted us to all drive out together."

"Where's she ... ? When's she ... ?"

"O'Hare. But I called a couple times and have been listening to the news. It's as crazy out there as it is here in the city. Most of the flights have been canceled or delayed. Last time I talked to her she had been on the Oklahoma City tarmac twice before they brought the plane back and canceled the flight. Forty and sunny in Oklahoma, a perfect day for flying and they can't take off because they have no place to land."

"I know that feeling," Jim said. "I love this weather. Lets you know that in the big scheme of things, we're squat."

"Sure, sure. That all your luggage?" Dan said pointing to the JCPenney's bag.

Jim nodded. "I'm beat. Where're we heading?"

"Hope you like plastic chairs. I told Alice we'd meet her at O'Hare, rain or shine—"

"Deep freeze or blizzard."

"The Buick's outside; if it hasn't been towed."

"That have an interior light?"

"What, are you kidding? It's loaded."

"I'll read you some poetry. Makes the time pass."

Dan led the way up two escalators to street level where pink streetlights bloodied the blanket of snow blowing horizontally. The cold pierced Jim's jacket and snow stuck to his close-cropped beard, whitening the gray hairs into an instant Santa Claus costume. When he spotted the bridge over the Chicago River, he paused.

"I remember that river from when I was a kid. It's smaller. But intense. It's a lot more intense."

"The car's parked a block north," Dan told him as they waited for the red light, the cars and buses in front of them skidding through the dirty slush of snow and ice.

They walked in silence through gray drifts until Dan broke toward what looked like an Indian burial mound that he then tried to unearth and unlock.

"I'll get her warmed up," Dan called, handing Jim a brush. "You try to free this baby."

The brush was useless in this snow. Jim swept his massive arm across the roof, the hood, then the trunk as the monster engine roared to life. "We're two now, buddy," Dan said, smiling, then put on his serious driver face when he slapped on his blinker and checked the traffic next to him.

"Flick on the interior light, Dan." Jim waved at the dashboard. "I can read you some Blake that will take your head off."

In the dim light, Jim read as they inched their way into the storm.

Chapter Three
TAKE OFF
Adrienne Lee

Chicago

"It feels good to be off that train," Jim said, drumming his open hand on the dashboard. Jim and Dan drove west up Monroe Street from Union Station, then pointed the Buick Wildcat northwest on the Kennedy expressway toward O'Hare airport.

The '68 Buick Wildcat was a grand car. Its powerful 455 cubic-inch engine had over 250,000 miles on it and hardly showed wear. Four-door, full power, red leather interior, wire wheel covers, dual exhaust, new Tiger Paw tires and a monster of a trunk. The dashboard was trimmed in faux Birdseye maple and sported a functioning 8-track player. Invariably, whenever he stopped for gas, someone would want to talk about the Buick. Dan would oblige, then politely refuse any and all offers to sell the old car.

"How about splitting some Chicago ribs? There's a rib place on Stony Island Drive, Funkys or Fluky's. We can swing in and get a brew."

"Let's not stop," Dan muttered. The falling snow was getting worse and traffic crawled around them. "We've got to get to the airport and meet up with Alice."

Jim punched the selector buttons of the radio and tuned to a rock station. For a moment, Dan wished he were alone, or traveling with Alice instead of Jim. He imagined Alice would be an ideal travel companion to California, keeping track of mileage and maps, being chatty then politely silent when they both needed to reflect. He imagined her handwriting, probably smooth and flowing. Her columns of numbers would be tight. He could see her adding up the expenses and tapping the edge of a silver mechanical pencil on her full lips. Pilots are like accountants. They always think in numbers, he mused. Yes, Alice would be the perfect travel companion.

Dan inched closer to a plow throwing sheets of snow to the side. With a little luck, they'd be at the airport in an hour. The sun was setting somewhere above the putty-colored snow clouds. Beautiful, he thought, but not good flying weather.

Oklahoma

Blood. Gallons of it, swirling pools of cardinal red that painted the walls of her mind and veiled her vision until that was all she could see.

Death seemed to pull her down. She almost welcomed it. Her thick long hair was wet now, circling around her split forehead. If she slipped into the water, she would die looking like a mermaid—all that swirling beautiful hair. She heard voices, muffled words. Flames of pain licked at her body. Cool blue, white-hot flames slid up her legs and threatened to envelop her. To drown or to burn to death. She must make a choice, now.

Then she heard the laughter. At first it was the merry sound of babies laughing, cooing and gurgling. Then it was children laughing as if they were skipping rope. Then it rose to a shrill and evil high pitch. She could feel the heat intensify now, her soft skin turning char colored in an instant. The pain, there was so much pain. Someone was pulling her up.

"You've got to help me. Pull! Pull now!" His nametag read "Charles Castro." His white flight attendant shirt repelled water like a wetsuit and glowed diaphanous in the dark. Alice wondered if he was called Chuck or Charlie. She grabbed his hand and screamed.

The scream escaped her hot, dry throat and reverberated through the bedroom. Alice's eyes flew open. Her heart was pounding in her ears and steamy-cold perspiration soaked her cotton nightgown. Arms still outstretched and frozen in mid-air, she clawed for breath.

"Good God in heaven, Charles," she gasped. She dreamed the same terror often, but never getting quite this far in her dream. Raking her fingers through damp hair, she patted the down comforter to reaffirm that she still had legs. Gradually the furniture became familiar. She sat up in bed getting her breath back, wringing her hands and calming tense stomach muscles. Alice had followed this routine since the crash. This time it was four-thirty in the morning. A lousy tradeoff.

Alice stared at the ceiling thinking about the blood and the flames of pain until she no longer feared the nightmare. Despite the months of therapy, she could feel tears welling up from within. She untangled her long legs from the comforter, stood up and sighed. *Red sky at morning*, she thought as she traced the rising Oklahoma sunrise on her window with her finger.

It could have been any other Tuesday, except she was flying to Chicago to visit her childhood friend, Opal, and to meet up with Dan and Jim.

Alice took a long shower, towel dried her straight black hair, and looked at her face in the mirror. Proud of her heritage as a Blackfoot Indian, she wished for the millionth time that her mother hadn't died in that car crash when she was a year old. The next seventeen years of being shuttled from one foster home to another had left their mark, most noticeably the pencil-thin scar above her right eye, always three shades lighter than her year-round tan complexion. She smiled as she touched it. Always getting in the middle of things, she thought and remembered the unfair fight between the older tough boy and the younger, gentler boy with curly black hair. She had stepped into the middle, was thrown back and fell directly onto the TV set's corner. She hadn't helped, but Jackson Opal became her life-long friend.

She threw herself into life the same way, working hard to escape poverty. Her search for stability led Alice to the Air Force. After twenty years she retired to fly commercially.

It could have been any other Tuesday. Alice eased the vintage Jaguar into the Tulsa Airport parking lot and gathered up her black leather briefcase and luggage. Hailing a shuttle, she settled into the green bench seat and stared out the window. Across the aisle sat a young family. The two little boys stared at her gold pilot wings. "Are you flying us to Detroit?" one asked.

"No, I'm flying other boys and girls to Chicago," Alice said, thinking about wind shifts, degrees and all the things that can go wrong during a routine flight. In the Air Force, she flew a C5A jet. Carrying people was different. It wasn't exciting, but her choices were slim after retirement—teaching, private pilot, commercial pilot or bum.

Now, as a commercial pilot, what did the future look like for her? She knew she shouldn't think about the letter to her and to the other crash survivors, warning them not to ever get together. Yet here she was, flying to Chicago to meet Jim and Dan. Get real, she admonished herself, how would anyone know what she was doing? There's no way; she was being ridiculous.

"Captain? We're here at TransAir now," the driver said, startling Alice out of her internal reverie; and she realized that she was now alone on the bus.

Gathering up her luggage, she stepped onto the center island dividing the lanes of fast-moving airport traffic. When a gap appeared, she glanced down and stepped off the curb. A taxi suddenly sped toward her. Alice lurched back toward the curb as she felt a force slam into her side. It wasn't the pain of speeding metal; it was the touch of saving flesh.

With a screech of tires, the taxi sped away.

"Are you all right?" She recognized Mike, a TransAir navigator. He stood over her, his hand extended.

"Shit! That goddamn idiot almost killed me." She stood.

"That was close. It was like he was aiming. Are you sure you're all right?"

"I'm fine. I really am. Next time I'll be more careful."

"Wasn't your fault, Captain." He shrugged. "I wish I'd gotten his license number."

Alice brushed dirt from her slacks as Mike escorted her across the street. Walking through the terminal, she glanced up at the CNN weather map and winced when they showed the Midwest cloaked by pockets of angry clouds from St. Louis to Cincinnati. She knew flights would be rerouted and cancelled in Tulsa. She stepped into an elevator.

"Wait, Captain! I'll ride with you."

Alice held the door as she turned to face her rescuer. "Thanks, Mike."

"I just found out, we're scheduled together today on 457 to O'Hare," he said. "I hope you like polka music and sauerbraten because we may have to settle for Milwaukee if the storm doesn't clear Chicago."

Alice studied his face and thought about how refreshing it was to be eager and full of life and promise. Doing the math, she realized that he, in his mid-twenties, could be her child.

"Thanks again," she said. "I owe you."

He smiled as they stepped off the elevator. "A navigator is supposed to protect his captain."

She used her security card to obtain access to the administration office of TransAir and pushed the heavy teak door open. The office was well appointed with models of current aircraft set in a display case. Posted in the corner of the large office, to the right of what pilots called The Big Sleep Lounge, were the flight schedules and personnel assignments. Alice dropped her luggage on a leather chair and signed in. She confirmed her flight pattern and made a mental note to send Mike a thank-you when she got back to Tulsa.

Minutes later, entering the 727, Alice handed her luggage to a flight attendant. "Can you get me some coffee, please, Fran?"

Fran hoisted the overstuffed bag and called over her shoulder, "Two creams and two sugars, right, Captain? And do you want grilled chicken or a club sandwich for dinner?"

Alice smiled. "Grilled chicken. Now let's see if we can get into O'Hare. There's a storm approaching Chicago." She settled into the pilot's seat, ran through her checklist, and took a moment to think about the near-accident. In the Air Force, you didn't think or question authority; you just stood in line for orders and meals. But the closeness of the taxi disturbed her. Mike was right; it did seem like the cab had intended to hit her. But why? She shook her head and finished the pre-flight checklist. With her headphones adjusted, Alice contacted the tower and idly watched the ground crew scurry around below the cockpit window.

Moments later, the tower contacted her. "TransAir four-fifty-seven, two-two left, Bravo Delta. Follow the Airbus."

"TransAir four-fifty-seven, two-two left, Bravo Delta," Alice confirmed. She drew a deep breath and looked toward the setting sun that turned the sky the color of orange sherbet. She remembered the beginning of that old saying, *Red sky at night, sailors' delight.*

At 33,000 feet, Alice thought of the rest: *Red sky in morning, sailors take warning.*

Chapter Four
AT O'HARE
Susan Kraykowski

Chicago

The phone beeped and Jackson Opal looked up from his neat stacks of supervisory reports. The screen identified Yolanda Barker from Scheduling as the caller. Jackson stretched a long arm to the phone, clearing his throat and putting a smile in his voice.

"How you doin' girlfriend? Ain't you off shift yet?" He did his best Queen Latifah impression. Yolanda always appreciated his voices. She answered in kind.

"Nawww. We on overtime now, honey. Relief can't get here through the snow. Maybe we sleep on cots tonight." Then seriously, "Jack, I just called to let you know Captain Alice's flight's delayed another hour."

"Shee-it"

"Sorry, Jackson. You know how it gets in a storm."

"Not your fault, Yo. Thanks for the head's up. You all take good care goin' home now, hear?" She tittered and rang off.

Jackson returned to the reports, filling in evaluations and occasionally checking his files and making further notations. The back of his mind filled with Alice, fighting her airplane through the storm, circling safe haven at the airport and unable to reach it for the time being.

Alice and me, fighting our way through shit since we were kids. Which foster home was it we met in? I couldn't have been more than seven, he thought.

Jackson recalled himself at that age, shuddering as he finished one report and began the next. He conjured fear, ready to cry at any moment, shocked by abuse and change and rootlessness almost beyond rescue. Six foster children in the Owlfeather home. Minnie Owlfeather, half Cherokee and half who–knew–what, mothered and monitored an ever-changing brood of children with learning disabilities, physical handicaps, juvenile records and mixed blood—the ones nobody else would take. The ones who had nowhere else to go.

It seemed to Jackson he'd been at Minnie Owlfeather's for a while, but the measurement of time had not been a solid concept for him then. Everything changed when Alice came, though. Sullen, hard, a few years older than he with a string of foster homes behind her, Alice had more or less adopted Jackson the moment she saw him. He followed her everywhere, trying to imitate her bravado, her toughness. He crawled into her bunk when the nightmares awakened him, sobbing and sweating.

"Shh, Jackson," she'd whispered. "I know all about it. You gotta fight back." More than anything he had wished he could fight back like Alice, wished he could be just like Alice.

As Jackson made his rounds, his walkie-talkie crackled to life.

"Opal," he answered.

"Jackson, it's Maria. You better come down here. We got a couple of locos on the moving sidewalk between B and C Concourses."

"What's so different about that?"

"They're causing a bottleneck."

"I'm thirty seconds away." As Jackson pushed past travelers on the escalator, he heard a stentorian voice declaim:

"Whilst Virtue is our walking-staff
And Truth a lantern to our path,
We can abide life's pelting storm
That makes our limbs quake, if our hearts be warm."

Jackson took the steps three at a time, dodging the carry-ons, parkas and toddlers. He threaded his way through a knot of travelers, frozen at the bottom of the escalator, staring ahead at the versifying moving walkway. Jackson focused on a silent man in a yellow sou'wester, staring at the synchronized neon lightshow above his head. Tinny strains of "Rhapsody in Blue" punctuated the poetry.

Maria materialized at Jackson's shoulder.

"Get everyone moving along the other side, okay?"

He turned to the crowd: "All right, folks. There's nothing to see here. Please follow the security guard." Maria smiled, beckoning the bewildered passengers. They began to shuffle after her, collecting carry-ons and kids, wheeling luggage and rubbernecking as long as possible.

Jackson approached the moving sidewalk and heard the dulcet, disembodied voice of the recording:

"The moving sidewalk is now ending. Please look down. The moving sidewalk is now ending . . ."

"Blow boisterous wind, stern winter frown . . ."

"Please look down. The moving . . ."

"Innocence is a winter's gown . . ."

"... ending. Please look down."

"So clad, we'll abide life's pelting storm That makes our limbs quake, if our hearts be warm."

"Please look down."

Seen closer, the man in the slicker was a dead ringer for the Gorton's fisherman. Jackson imagined him planted solidly on deck in his rubber boots, fish guts sloshing about his ankles.

Behind the fisherman, the poetry issued from a large man in an olive-drab jacket. He was bent over, snatching scattered pages and stuffing them into a shopping bag.

So here's our other loco. Great, the Gorton's Fisherman lands Charlie the Tuna. Why do people get so wiggy when the weather's bad, Jackson thought as he assumed a nonthreatening stance.

Jackson uncorked a professional smile. "Gentlemen ... may I offer assistance?"

Fisherman looked behind him and nudged his companion. "Jim. Stand up."

"I don't care if it's the feds, Dan. I gotta get my Blake."

All three men stooped down to grab the last few pages off the end of the sidewalk. Dan stood up and said, "We're waiting for a friend whose flight's delayed and thought we'd come down here to see the light show." His attention wavered off to the side wall where pastel lights played across wavy glass tiles—the ocean at dawn.

"May I escort you somewhere? Perhaps to your gate or the Information Center?"

Gorton Fisherman and Charlie the Tuna shouldered around Jackson as though he were a ceiling support that happened to block their way. "Why do you suppose they chose 'Rhapsody in Blue,' Jim?"

"Well, they were two of the least troublesome crazies we've had in a while," Jackson duly finished his shift-change report to his relief man amid the commotion of evening security staff coming on duty, and day staff going off duty. He shouldered his gym bag and left the nondescript office through a back hallway. As he walked, he loosened his regulation red tie with one hand.

A bit further on, Jackson merged with O'Hare's many travelers—some harried and annoyed, some resigned or nervous, some of them stupid. He sidestepped several who had stopped in the middle of the flow, others eddying and backing up behind them. He picked out the ones who would cause trouble—nothing more serious than whining about whether their film will be affected by the X-rays or trying to send a baby carrier through on the conveyor belt without removing the baby. Some day, he thought, I'll write a book—*"Through O'Hare Security with Gun and Camera"*—a best seller.

He glanced at a monitor as he passed. Alice's flight from Oklahoma City hadn't changed ETA or gate since Yolanda's call. About twenty minutes before it lands, and perhaps another ten or fifteen minutes until the crew leaves the plane. Plenty of time to freshen up. Jackson used his passkey to unlock an unused storage closet. The overhead light came on as he entered. He dropped his gym bag and locked the door.

From the gym bag, Jackson removed a smaller bag, a padded hanger and another set of hangers with garments carefully covered in plastic and folded to minimize wrinkles. These he hung on a hook, first shaking the wrinkles out. Then he kicked off his loafers and unbuckled the belt of his gray uniform trousers, removing his wallet from the hip pocket and his keys from the right side. He placed wallet and keys in a zippered compartment in the gym bag, then shucked his slacks and hung them on the padded hanger, fussy about the crease. His navy-blue blazer followed, along with the tie. His shirt, socks and briefs would go in the laundry later; he didn't worry about folding them.

He pulled a lighted magnifying mirror from the small bag and lined up a cordless electric razor, concealer, base, blush, eye shadow and mascara on the shelf next to it, examining his complexion critically. As he shaved, his thoughts returned to Alice and how nice it would be to see her again, even if it was only for one night. Ah, Alice, you'll probably want to steal my new skirt, you heartless bitch.

Twenty minutes later, Jackson gave himself a thorough inspection, added cinnamon-colored lipstick and zipped up the gym bag. He bounced a bit to settle the falsies and smoothed his black skirt over his rump. Jackson Opal entered the closet a security supervisor; he exited as Opal Jackson, model.

Terminal 2, Gate G18—it would be all the way at the end. Damn long walk in heels. Plenty of time though. Alice should just be completing her final trip check. We can take the "L" into town and go to dinner, just girls out for fun. No problems with snow when there's rapid transit. Pity the poor suburban slobs who have to drive. Plenty of crumpled passengers coming this way. Must have been a hell of a flight. They're what? Three-and-a-half hours late? Could be worse, folks, could be worse. You all go along and find out your connections are canceled and have a nice night on the cots in the concourse. We'll watch you on the ten o'clock news.

Opal strutted along the concourse, running the internal monologue and tossing back her springy black hair. A number of men, tired as they were, did double takes. With her high cheekbones, pert derrière and café au lait complexion, Opal under full sail seemed to draw them into her wake. They followed her hungrily with their eyes and sighed as they turned toward the baggage claim and their wives waiting in SUVs out at the chaotic curbside.

As Opal approached Gate G18, expecting to find the waiting area deserted, she stopped dead in her tracks. Oh, for all the oil in Oklahoma. It would have to be Gorton's Fisherman and Charlie the Tuna. *Alice* is the friend they're waiting for? Jackson paused. Shit, now it makes sense. Good thing I changed.

Alice appeared at the jet way door, pulling her wheeled suitcase. "Opal!" She shared a secret grin with her lifelong friend. "Jim and Dan!" Dan stepped in front of Opal to hug Alice. As Dan stepped back from Alice's comforting hug, she caught Opal and air-kissed her cheek.

"It's great to see you. Have you all met yet?"

Jim enfolded Alice in a tremendous bear hug.

"No, we haven't met your friend, Alice." Gorton Fisherman turned to regard Opal and glanced away, blushing.

"Opal Jackson is my oldest and dearest friend. Opal, this is Dan O'Keefe and Jim Brill. They were on the De Havilland that crashed."

Opal allowed Jim to engulf her hand in his, looking into his brown eyes and feeling as though he looked right through her.

Opal turned to Dan and smiled.

Dan shook her hand. "Uh ... how do you do?"

"Alice has told me a lot about you." She glanced at Alice. "So, what's the plan?" No one answered. "What about dinner? Alice and I usually go downtown when she's here on a layover."

Alice began to wheel her suitcase along the concourse and the others trooped along in a loose pod.

"I've got the Buick here," Dan offered. "We could get started right away."

"Yeah! What about some Southside ribs? I know this place, Fluky's or Flakie's ... Funky's—"

"I had in mind someplace a bit closer to my apartment. I'm in Laketown." Opal cut him off, not in the least eager to escort Alice's honkies south of McCormack Place in a snowstorm. "Do you have a place to stay?"

"Uh, no. We didn't plan for that."

"Look. All of you come to my place. Spend the night. We'll grab take-out and you can get some rest and start in the morning after the plows have been out."

"Opal, are you sure?" Alice's question carried its secret message of concern. "It's an imposition. We could put up where the flight crews stay."

"Are you crazy, girlfriend? With the storm, every hotel in twenty miles is booked solid, and you know it. The boys can sleep in the living room. We'll sleep in the bedroom. Why don't you go on ahead on the train and pick up some dinner? You know how to get to my place. I'll creep along the Kennedy with these boys and show them the way."

"Thanks, Opal. You're the best."

"Alice? Could I ride the train with you?" Jim asked. "I used to live in Chicago. It would be fun to ride the 'L' again."

"Yeah, sure. Come on," she said hoping not to sound too eager. Then she indicated the escalator down toward baggage claim and stepped on ahead of everyone else. She looked back up the staircase at Opal, Dan and Jim on the highest step.

In the labyrinth beneath O'Hare, Alice and Jim turned into the CTA terminus, waving to Opal and Dan. Alice supplied the tokens and the train departed almost as soon as she and Jim were seated. They traveled in personal, but not environmental silence as the overheated car rattled and roared on its icy tracks. Jim stared out the window at the frozen river of taillights on the tollway and the oncoming glacier of headlights on the Kennedy Expressway.

At the Irving Park stop, Jim reached into his JCPenney's bag and pulled out a tattered volume. He started organizing the loose pages. "Do you read Blake, Alice?"

"You're a student of poetry?"

"It's all here. Life, death and everything in between." He let the book fall open to "Songs of Innocence." The doors to the car whooshed closed and the train rattled toward the Loop again, the streetlights along the expressway hazed the snow in a nimbus of orange light.

"I prefer Whitman myself. The bard of the American experience, the body electric."

"Contemporaries. I like Whitman, too."

"Do you write poetry?"

"Well ... some."

"Well ... can I hear some?"

"No."

"Oh, come on! I love the idea that people can make things up right out of their heads. Come on. Just one?"

Jim stared at her and then, without reference to his book or papers, recited:

Apocalypse
Around the sun a ring is formed and round
The ring appears a power shaped like God.
The constellations tremble from the sound
Of russet, days-end bells which start to nod.
Behind the power rests a long, tall cloud
Which cancerous grows and churns as it expands.
Its burly strength humiliates the proud
And havoc roams at will throughout the land.
In agony the oceans retch and groan
And huddle terror-filled within their bowls.
The poisoned wind collapses with a moan
To seek a quiet bed among dry shoals.
For those with dry feet there's no longer room.
The red bells clang and sound a ghastly doom.

Chapter Five

THE WATCHER

Kim Dechert

Chicago

Brad watched from his apartment window as the couple trudged up the snowy sidewalk, heads bent low, clutching paper bags to their chests. Swirling snow whipped around them, but the hulk of the man stepped surefooted. Brad immediately recognized the slim figure wearing her blue uniform under a white parka, her arm looped through the man's. But who was the guy?

He stepped away from the window and stared at the wall clock. Its interminable ticking reminded him time was running out. He turned back to the window and took another long, hard look. The size, the walk. Then it hit him. Jim Brill? My God. Why are they together? Brad's features distorted in a grimace. He cracked his knuckles and waited.

"Whew," said Alice, entering the apartment building, and stomping her boots on the rubber mat. "At last!" She pressed the numbered keys in the sequence she remembered and the lobby door opened.

"We've got one hell of a Chicago blizzard!" Jim said, brushing snow off his beard.

Alice walked toward the stairs. "Come on, Opal's apartment's on the second floor."

Jim followed enjoying the view of Alice in her neat, form-fitting uniform slacks. He imagined her in bed, rumpled and warm, waking up to a kiss.

Inside Opal's apartment, Alice hung their coats in the closet. Jim stood in the middle of the foyer holding the dinners, watching her. He'd never met anyone quite like her. So different from Juliana.

The phone rang. "Oh, I hope they haven't gotten stuck somewhere," Alice said, hurrying to the telephone. "Jim, take the food to the kitchen; it's down the hall on your right. I'll get the phone." Certain it was Opal, she lifted the receiver. "Opal?"

The man's voice surprised her. "No, it's Brad. Is that you, Alice? Is everything okay?"

Alice paused, "It's me, Brad. Why do you think something's wrong?"

"I saw you outside with some guy. I got concerned."

Alice frowned. What an ass. She couldn't believe how nosy he was. "Don't worry Brad, everything's fine."

"Is Opal there?"

"No," Alice didn't care if she sounded abrupt.

"I figured the airport would be closed."

Trying to cut it short, Alice was all business. "I'll tell Opal you called."

"Are you visiting for long?"

God, this guy wouldn't give it up. "No, we're leaving in the morning." Damn, she shouldn't have said anything; he'd keep her on the line forever. "Gotta go, Brad."

"Tell Opal to call me the minute she gets in."

"I'm not sure how late she'll be, Brad. And we're leaving first thing tomorrow."

"Leaving? The airport won't be open that soon with this much snow. Is Opal going?"

"No, just me and my friends. We're heading for California."

"My mother lives in California." Brad's nasal voice irritated Alice and she bit her tongue to keep from being rude. "Just tell Opal I called." Brad broke the connection.

As Alice hung up the phone, she shivered with the memory of her last encounter with Brad. TransAir had canceled her flight from Chicago; and Opal was working an evening shift. She knew Brad was a neighbor of Opal's and had chitchatted with him in the elevator several times before. That night she was famished. Dreading the sight of Opal's chronically empty refrigerator, she had accepted his offer to dinner at Bistro 110, one of her favorite restaurants just off Michigan Avenue.

Brad seemed pleasant enough at dinner and insisted on buying an expensive Merlot once he knew her wine preference.

Back at Opal's apartment, she opened the door and turned to give Brad a friendly peck on the cheek. He suddenly turned his head and kissed her hard, grabbing her hips and shoving her against the wall. One hairy hand was fumbling with her blouse buttons before she surfaced from her shock, stiffened and pushed at his chest. Brad just held her tighter, slobbering down her neck.

"Let me go now or your family jewels will be ground glass," Alice yelled, raising one knee. Brad jerked back, apologized and quickly left.

Alice still had no use for him. I wonder why Opal puts up with such an asshole, she thought. She found Jim in the kitchen, his head buried in the refrigerator. "There's usually some diet pop. I'm sure Opal won't mind if you help yourself. Plates are in the cabinet over there, napkins in that basket," she pointed. "Go ahead and start if you're hungry."

Jim grabbed two beers and popped one open, offering it to Alice. "It's been a while since we shared a cold one." He shook his head. "A jar of pickles, eggs, a half bag of Oreos. Reminds me of my fridge at home."

She crossed her arms. "Yeah, well, Opal's busy and doesn't cook much."

Jim laughed. "Me neither. I've got better things to do with my time." Instead of opening his own beer, he stepped closer to Alice, framed her face with his hands and gently kissed her. She deepened the kiss.

Brad stood at his window and watched the snow continue to pile up. He never prayed in his life, but suddenly he had the urge to thank the heavens for delivering Jim Brill to his doorstep. After so much that had gone wrong, he felt it was about time he got a break. He remembered the day of the plane crash. If Jim had died as he was supposed to, the payoff would have been big, really big. There wouldn't be snow outside his window; there'd be palm trees and white sandy beaches.

"Damn!" he said aloud, remembering all the money he had to borrow when he should have been spending it without a care. He thought of the almost daily phone calls from his pushy loan officers who said his time was running out.

The '68 Buick pulling into the lot across the street caught his attention. He recognized Opal as soon as she stepped out. He assessed the guy with her—Dan? This was too good to be true.

"Hey, girlfriend, we're home," Opal called from the front hall. Alice and Jim sprang apart and quickly straightened their clothes. They turned toward the refrigerator, reaching for more drinks and trying to hide their flushed faces.

While the weary foursome ate, Alice mentioned Brad's telephone call. "He called?" Opal asked, her voice tight.

"I couldn't get him off the phone, so I told him we were taking off early in the morning. Sorry, should've kept my mouth shut. He's creepy, Opal."

Jim looked up from his meal. "Who is this Brad guy?"

"Lives across the hall," Opal offered. "The longer I know him, the less I like him. But I better call him back." Opal pushed away from the table and grabbed the phone, leaving the others to clean up. "While you're on your way to sunny California, he'll be here with me."

"Lucky you," Alice said.

"Better turn in soon," Dan said. "We need to be fresh in the morning. The roads are still bad. Even if the snow stops, it'll be crap driving."

Hanging up the phone, Opal clapped her hands and started organizing the sleeping arrangements. She was in her element—loved orchestrating, especially as Opal. "All right, boys, let's get these sheets on the sofa. And I have an extra sleeping bag one of you can use."

Later, Alice sat on the bed in her nightgown as she watched Opal remove her makeup.

"Brad's mother is in bad shape, I guess. He said he'd be taking off tomorrow to be with her. He actually sounded sad," Opal said.

"I don't care," Alice said. "There's just something about him."

Opal gingerly pulled the pins out around her scalp as the wig gave way to close-cropped hair. "Alice, let's face it, he's trouble." He looked at her in the mirror. "Want something in my closet?"

Alice looked up. "Really Jackson, anything?" As Jackson nodded, Alice jumped off the bed, heading to the closet. "Hmmm, where's that little black skirt you were wearing tonight?"

"You mean this one?" He held up the skirt in front of him, swishing his hips and the skirt at the same time in some sort of bullfighter's dance. "Ha, I had a feeling you were feasting your eyes on this little number. Coco Chanel, wool with a silk lining, utterly delicious. It's all yours." He tossed it to her.

"You're a real pal, Jackson Opal."

Brad stared at the clock. Maybe now he was on track to his well-deserved moment in the sun. The memories of the last two years ripped through him. It had been hell. He realized he should never have borrowed the money. But now that didn't matter. Soon he wouldn't have to worry. After services were rendered, payday wouldn't be far off. He began packing the smallest suitcase he owned. The warmth of California would feel good, assuming he got that far.

It was still dark when Dan pulled the Buick in front of the apartment building. The freshly plowed roads looked icy and ominous in the glare of the streetlight. They had decided not to wake Opal, but left a note. Jim jumped into the car first, deciding to ride shotgun with map in hand and his JCPenney's bag close to his feet. Alice stretched out in the backseat.

As they were about to pull away, someone knocked on Jim's window. He rolled it down. Brad stood there. "Room for one more?" he asked. No one spoke. He looked at Alice. "It's my mother. I have to get to her, and O'Hare's closed."

She hesitated and saw Dan shrug. "Okay," she said, regretting the decision the second it left her mouth. Gritting her teeth, she moved over. Brad quickly got in the backseat, placing his suitcase between him and Alice.

They rode in silence until the city's skyline faded into hints of dawn. Dan focused on the road, cautious about slick spots. Alice couldn't wait to tell Opal about Brad. Jim tried to stay awake, but his eyes began to droop, the rural scenery lulling him to sleep. The last thing he remembered was a farm with a huge blue and white billboard proclaiming, "Home of 'Nappy' Prized Miniature Horse."

Chapter Six
THE BUFFALO CAVE
Kitty Jarman

Illinois

Alice saw the billboard too. Nappy. What a great name for a horse. She'd worked with ponies as a rodeo clown during the summer she turned eighteen. The experience helped her survive.

Alice brought herself back to the present as Dan maneuvered the Buick carefully through the I-90 Exit Ramp onto Randall Road west of Elgin.

Glancing at Brad, watching him fall into an easy sleep, she wondered, how did this happen? Snow fluttered against the car window. Then scenes from the plane crash played in her mind. Tears stung her eyes. No, she decided, I'm not going to think about any of it right now. She reached into her leather handbag and pulled out the Armani lotion Opal had given her. It felt smooth and silky on her dry hands. It reminded her of the scent of Jim's cologne. Sexy, she thought.

The night before in Opal's apartment, Alice, Dan and Jim worked on the safest route to California. Between somber discussions about Charles dying, Dan said he preferred to stay off interstate routes because of the car's age. "That's one reason," Jim said, avoiding what they all thought.

Only Alice had the courage to say it. "We don't want to be seen. The letter said it's dangerous for us to be together. We can cross the Mississippi into Iowa. It's off the beaten path. No one in their right mind would take that route to California."

After the guys went to bed, Alice turned to her friend for advice. "Opal, take off your garter belt and put on your security hat. Does this zigzag route make sense?"

"Sounds great to me," Opal agreed. "Anyone looking for the likes of you will be searching the Quad Cities or the St. Louis bypass. Watch your butt, now. I won't be there."

"You're always with me in spirit." Alice hugged her old friend. The rest of the evening was uneventful, except for their excited whispers as they admired Opal's latest fashion finds.

The snow had let up a little, but the sky was still the shade of Pennsylvania slate. After a while Dan called out, "We must have passed a million churches on this road."

Jim, fidgeting in the front passenger seat, turned to look through the back window. He started singing, "Stopped into a church," from *California Dreaming*.

Dan ignored him and checked the rearview mirror, easing the car into the right lane. "Should we make a pit stop before I turn onto Route sixty-four or wait until we hit the Mississippi?"

"Let's wait." Jim closed his ratty Blake book. "We can stop at White Pines near the Rock River."

"White Pines near the Rock River. Sounds like a band," Dan laughed.

"Let's stop now," said Alice, "I really have to go."

When the Buick pulled into a gas station, Alice slung her leather bag over her shoulder. "Want anything?"

"A pack of spearmint gum, Alice." Jim held out a dollar bill.

She ignored it, walking into the gas station, digging into the bottom of her purse for her cell phone. After two rings, Opal picked up.

"Hey girlfriend."

"Alice, I've been worried sick. Why didn't you wake me?"

"We kept you up late enough, no reason to wake you early. The snow is actually letting up a little here."

"Where's here?"

"The boonies."

"It's coming down harder than ever in the city. Good thing you left so early. They closed the Kennedy a half hour ago."

"Well. I would say my luck is changing, except for Brad."

"What about Brad?"

"He's with us. Tapped on the car window as we were leaving. His mom is dying."

"Brad is with you now?" Alice heard a sharp intake of breath, then a quiet, "Fuck."

"Opal?"

"Um, sorry, Alice, I just spilled coffee on my new nighty. How the hell did he get into the picture?"

"Brad? He wanted a ride to a city with an airport that's open. I almost felt sorry for him."

"Shit Alice, I don't like him being there. You guys are under enough pressure. Call me whenever you get a chance, okay? Damn it."

"God, Opal, let's not get anal. We're just giving your neighbor a ride."

"Alice," Jackson dropped his voice. "You're all in danger. The fewer people that know, the better. Remember the letter?"

"Jackson?" Alice picked up on his switch in voice.

"Yeah, it's me. Don't get to talk to me very often any more do you? Listen to me sweetheart, just be careful. Security is my business, you know?"

"Yeah, well, once we get out there and talk to Charles we're all going to be glad it's over."

"Just don't forget to duck, Alice. Remember when we played Duck, Duck, Goose?"

"Yeah, sure, and I love you too, Opal Jackson."

Alice clicked off the phone and headed for the counter to buy a pack of gum. Handing it to Jim, she noticed he held her hand a second longer than necessary. Then she climbed into the backseat and smiled.

As the Buick headed toward the Mississippi River, Jim fiddled with radio dials finding only static. Dan reached over and smacked Jim's hand. "Enough!"

Jim pretended to pout. "Are we there yet?" Dan laughed as he glanced in the rearview mirror at Brad who slept with his head propped against Alice's pillow.

They traveled in quiet for a while, then Alice leaned forward and whispered into Jim's ear, "Hey, Jimbo, what did you think when you got the letter?"

He held her hand then brought it to his lips. "To hell with the letter."

The car suddenly jerked sideways. Alice reached out to brace herself, then turned to stare at Dan who spoke through clenched teeth. "Leave it alone, Alice."

"Why? We've already decided to risk it all. Isn't that why we're on this trip?"

"We shouldn't be talking about this, Alice." Dan hissed, looking back at Brad, "I don't want anything to happen."

Several miles passed as the three survivors watched the frozen Midwest roll by the steaming windows of the Buick. Alice used her index finger to trace their names in her foggy side window. "Dan, what did you think when you got the letter?"

Keeping his eyes on the snow-covered road ahead, Dan sighed, "We shouldn't be talking about this. Drop it, Alice."

Jim turned and looked at Brad to confirm he was still asleep. "Remember where we were three weeks after the crash?"

"In Chicago," Dan slowed down to take a sharp right. "We were on the Magnificent Mile, as I recall." He drove carefully around a snowdrift and continued his sentence. "Michigan Avenue, listening to the voice from hell."

"Yeah, the devil himself," Jim added his two cents.

Silence hung in the car as they drove toward the deathbed of a man who had first saved their lives, then filled it with terror. Charles had arranged for the survivors to meet at Rod's real estate office on Michigan Avenue.

Alice played absently with her bracelet. "My God, I remember how devastated Charles looked when he heard that damn tape. It scared the hell out of me."

"What I remember is that my room at the Hyatt was first class," Jim laughed. "I sure enjoyed that hot tub, though I didn't remember much after the third tequila."

"Seriously, Jim. I think we were in shock," Alice replied. "Especially when Charles told us about his dog's death. An accident? Yeah, right, like dog shootings happen in ritzy neighborhoods everyday."

Jim interrupted. "Charles wanted to find out who was on the plane and why. When he started tracking things down, suddenly the dog got killed."

Dan continued. "I remember Charles telling us the voice on the cassette tape was the same voice on the telephone telling him his dog was the first one. The voice said it wasn't an accident."

"He looked devastated," Alice said softly.

"All I know is the voice on the tape gave me the willies." Dan slowly repeated the words they all remembered:

"This is not your game. One word and everyone you know is dead. Everyone. You get a second chance at life and the only cost is silence."

Dan turned down the car's heater. "When Charles urged us to move on, leave things alone, it made sense."

"And then there's obtuse Rod," Jim mumbled, drumming his fingers on the dashboard.

"Rod seemed numb to it all," said Dan. "I left a message and told him we were driving to California to see Charles, but he never called back."

"Of course," Jim said. "The guy's got nothing to say."

Two years ago, they had returned to what had been their lives before the crash, Jim without his wife. Then, just as they started to believe Charles had been making a mountain out of a molehill, the threatening letter arrived.

Alice leaned forward between the men. "It's the last sentence," she mused. "The one that keeps bouncing around in my mind."

"Me too," said Dan. "But why Latin?" He recited the words. *"In nubibus, inter canem et lupum est licentia vatum."*

Alice touched Jim's hand. "What do you think it means?"

"Damned if I know."

Dan raised his voice, "Just what the hell do you think happened? What caused the plane to crash that day? Do you think Charles has any idea? Maybe that's why he wants us there."

Alice leaned back massaging her temples. "Oh God, Dan, who knows. I'm sorry I brought it up. I'm gonna nap for a while. Wake me up when we get to the Mississippi."

The Buick sailed along the Rock River while Jim read his William Blake. In the backseat, Alice closed her eyes savoring the feeling of being with Jim and Dan. She'd been alone for a long time between lovers. She enjoyed the attention of the two men. Both good looking, but Jim was the one she wanted.

"'Tyger, Tyger, burning bright.'" He turned and smiled at her.

She loved his smile. Alice wrapped her mother's hand-woven shawl around her. It was always with her, the only thing she had from her past. Alice searched for her pillow and then glanced at Brad. "That bastard got my pillow." She jerked it out from under him and stuffed it between the door and her head, ignoring Brad's mumbling. Slowly she drifted into a troubled sleep.

Forty miles from the Mississippi, the Buick hit a bump.

She awoke suddenly, lying face down, nose imbedded in fur. She was clinging to the back of a large animal moving beneath her. Multiple grunts and snorts filled the otherwise quiet air. Lifting her head slowly, she glanced around. Yes, she was riding on the back of a bison. They were at the edge of a herd traveling over small hills and valleys. Dewdrops gathered on top of tall grasses. Puffy white clouds scattered, condensed, then scattered again in a powder-blue sky. There was a dreamy quality about the landscape. Somehow understanding that she was in no danger, she laid her head back on the hairy pillow.

By afternoon, her body had molded itself to the buffalo's broad back. Every movement he made, she reciprocated and matched with her flesh. She was participating in the rhythm of life. Her right hand reached down to touch herself. After a few moments, she felt the spasm of an orgasm rack her body as she clutched a fistful of fur. Beneath her, the large bison snorted. A strong musky scent rose above his thick hairy legs.

She continued the ride in silence until the sun hung low. Suddenly chilled, she groaned aloud. "What the hell am I doing here?" At the sound of her voice, the large animal strode toward an outcropping of rock. He tipped ever so slowly, allowing her to slide off his back to the ground.

Alice noticed a small cave cut into the side of a hill. Entering cautiously, she discovered a wood fire and several buffalo hides. Settling beneath the hides, she watched as smoke found its way into the cracks and crevices above. The cave seemed familiar. Drawings on the wall danced in the flickering firelight. Rising slowly, she moved closer to decipher the pictures. Before she could make any sense out of the childish scribbling, she heard the buffalo moving just outside the opening of the cave. Leaning forward, straining to read the mysterious message, she was interrupted by a familiar voice.

She stirred and pulled her mother's shawl closer.

"Hey, Alice are you up? The voice belonged to Brad, wide awake and smiling. She refused to return his smile. What was I dreaming about, Alice thought as she turned to look out the window. The snow had stopped and the sun peeked through the gray sky. The dream's eerie essence hung near her, but she remembered only the cave, and the feeling of riding that magnificent animal. Something is missing. Something dark and important. She focused on the back of Jim's head.

Iowa

Less than an hour later, Dan was still at the wheel. The Buick traveled through the back roads in blinding snow-filled silence. When they neared an unnamed town, Alice became more unsettled. She couldn't throw off the haunting feeling of the dream.

"Let's stop and eat," Jim suggested as they neared a Burger King.

In the restroom, Alice splashed cold metallic water onto her face. Searching her reflection in the murky mirror, her mind played back the dream. One of the drawings had looked like a crumpled airplane. Next to it were five stick figures walking west toward a setting sun. One held something in its hand and looked back at a longhaired figure standing to the side. However, it was the banner beneath the drawing that made her blood freeze. Written in bold letters were the words: *"In nubibus, inter canem et lupum est licentia vatum."* Her eyes widened and she understood.

"In the clouds between the dog and the wolf, is the license allowed to poets."

Chapter Seven

THE STARS THROW DOWN THEIR SPEARS

Kevin Burris

Iowa

"It's fucking freezing out here." Dan lipped a cigarette and cupped his lighter with a gloveless hand.

Jim nodded, pulling his collar up over unprotected ears. "That's 'cause there's nothing between us and the Rockies to stop the north wind, sport." He stamped his feet as Dan took a deep drag and let the smoke go.

Dan glanced at Alice huddled next to Jim on the rusted corpse of a broken chaise lounge, and felt a stab of jealousy. "So," he said after a minute of staring into the snow-filled swimming pool, "Is there some reason we need to be here, sweetheart? I mean other than maybe you think we might need to brush up on our ice water survival skills?"

"Funny." Alice smirked into her fur-lined hood.

"Well, I mean you must have a reason for calling this meeting."

"God, look at the stars!" Jim said, his hands jammed in his pockets as he stared straight up.

"That's why." Alice replied.

Dan drew on the Marlboro again, "What's why?"

"I had a dream. In the car, before. I had a dream."

Jim looked back down from the stars and over at Dan, who returned the glance. They both paused for a moment before Dan spoke again. "Excuse me there, captain, but the rest of your flight crew here seems to be having some difficulty following."

Alice didn't answer.

"Well, let me be more specific then. It's twenty-seven degrees; it's one in the morning. We have perfectly good rooms in the best Lucky 8 motel west of Cedar Rapids, but instead we're standing on the frozen pool deck in the wind because you want to discuss exactly what, your dreams?"

"Geez, we're a little crabby aren't we?" Jim smiled, moving closer to Alice.

Dan flicked an ash. "Well I'd be a lot less crabby if I hadn't just driven thirteen hours to find they don't have a fucking bar in the hotel we finally stop at. And by the way . . ." He jerked a thumb back toward Brad's second-floor non-smoking room, "No matter what sleeping beauty up there says, tomorrow we are definitely not taking the Interstate. We're staying with our plan."

Jim rested a hand on Alice's shoulder. "We'll see. So what's up?" he asked softly. "You were saying something about the stars?"

Alice shifted her position ever-so-slightly toward the comforting hand. "In the car today, I had a dream about the crash. It was odd. Different."

"Shit," Dan said, "we ALL have dreams about the crash. Some of us have them every damn night."

Jim nodded agreement.

"I know, I know," Alice continued. "But this was something different, new. This was something real."

She had his attention. "What do you mean real?" Dan asked, flipping a butt into the pool.

"There was an old cave. An Indian cave. There was a drawing inside."

Jim tilted his head. "You mean like one of those caves in France? Caveman caves with the drawings of animals and stuff?"

"Yes, pictographs, but not there, not in Europe. It was right here in America."

Dan pulled his ski cap snug, fished inside his jacket for another cigarette. "Okay, so you had a dream about a cave. What's that got to do with the crash?"

Alice looked up at him from inside her hood. "The drawing on the cave wall was a representation of the airplane, of the crash and the wreckage, of us, of the survivors."

Dan stopped fumbling with his cigarette pack. "Alice," he said, shivering and searching for his lighter, "it's not getting any warmer out here."

Jim waved Dan off. "Easy, Dan. Easy. Let her finish."

But Dan growled. "Finish what? She had a dream. Just a dream of an old cave with a picture she thinks is an airplane. So what? No offense, but what does this have to do with anything real?"

Alice threw back her hood and stared straight at Dan. "It is real. It's as real as this fucking cold. As real as the fact that the airplane crashed and people died."

Dan stopped searching for his lighter, stunned by her sudden intensity.

"Whoa, whoa, Alice" Jim said softly after a moment. "Start over. Slowly. You're talking about a prehistoric cave with a drawing of our airplane in it. With a drawing of us in it. And you're saying that this cave exists. It's a real thing?"

Alice continued to stare straight at Dan. "Yes."

"Where is it?"

"Out west, maybe Oklahoma. I'm not sure." She looked away. "I'll know it when I see it. I'll know the place, know the country."

Dan found his composure and his lighter and another cigarette. "Well, that narrows things down."

"Shut up, Dan," Jim snapped without looking at him. He spoke to Alice, "Go on, what were you saying about stars before?"

"In the drawing, there are stars. There is a sun and the five survivors are walking toward it. One of the survivors is looking back at the crash. He's holding something in his hand."

"What? What's he holding?" Jim asked, gently coaxing.

"I don't know. I can't tell. I mean it's a pictograph. Everything is a representation. I just know that it's important. It's something we need to find."

"Anything else?" Jim asked rocking back.

"Yes, there's an inscription in Latin."

Dan paced and smoked at the pool edge. "Now just a minute. This doesn't make sense. I mean you've got a prehistoric cave. What's that, twenty- to thirty-thousand-years old with a picture of an airplane in it, and an inscription in Latin? You're all over the map, Alice. Geographically, historically. None of this makes any sense. It's a dream. It was just a dream."

"No."

45

Dan shook his head. "Alice, I love you, babe, but this is nuts. I'm going in."

As he started to walk past her she reached out and grabbed his wrist. "No, please," she said.

"I'm sorry, but I'm freezing my chance for children off out here. What you're saying makes no sense. It can't be real."

"It is. I swear it is." She looked up into his face, pleading.

"Ok, how do you know?"

"I was there, *dammit*. It seemed so real."

"When were you there, Alice? When?"

"Today, I was there today." They paused for a long moment looking deep into each other's eyes.

Slowly Dan placed a gloved hand over hers. He glanced at Jim who met the look without a word. "I'm sure you were," he said finally, squeezing her hand and moving toward the motel. "I'll see you inside."

Alice and Jim sat back-to-back in silence for several minutes after Dan had gone.

"You must think I've gone crazy," she said at last.

"The stars throw down their spears," Jim replied, gazing into the star-bright sky. After a moment, "What does it say?"

"The inscription?"

"Yes, tell me."

"I don't speak Latin."

"But you know what it says?"

"Yes."

"Tell me," he repeated.

Alice took a deep breath before answering. Jim leaned softly into her. "In the clouds," she said, "between the dog and the wolf, is the license allowed to poets." She laughed and then sighed. "I have no idea what it all means."

Jim turned and put an arm around her. "You see that star up there, the bright one?" he whispered, pointing.

"Yes."

"That's Sirius. The brightest star in the sky. One of the closest. The Dog star."

Alice sat up suddenly, turning to him, eyes wide. "I remember that. And the wolf?"

"Lupus is hidden below the horizon. It's a southern constellation."

"And the clouds, Jim? What about the clouds between?"

"See for yourself," he smiled, tracing the wide swath of the Milky Way with his hand.

Suddenly her eyes brimmed. "Thank you, Jim," she whispered. "Thank you."

He kissed her. She leaned into him and they snuggled warm and silent for a long time beneath the bright canopy of winter stars.

Chapter Eight
CONNECTIONS
Mike Balcom-Vetillo

Iowa

Transient light escaped from the motel lobby, touched the broken sidewalk and reflected off the flickering Pepsi machine just outside the door. The light stretched to the chain-link fence surrounding the snowy swimming pool, but dimmed before reaching Alice and Jim. For the moment they lived in darkness, unaware of Brad's gaze as he leaned near the isolated black wall phone, rummaging through his front jeans pocket for a piece of paper.

Feeling the worn edge, he pulled it out, read the scribbled, smudged number, and dialed. Somewhere in Chicago, a phone rang once, twice, three times. Counting, Brad squinted to sharpen his view. Silhouetted against the distant glow of the Sioux City horizon, Jim and Alice, silent in their pose, leaned close to each other.

No answer. Brad hung up in frustration. His stomach twisted. He considered leaving, running away from it all, away from the familiar nervousness pulling at his gut since the crash. He dialed again. It rang once.

"Hello?"

"I thought she was supposed to be dead."

"Where the hell have you been, Brad? I haven't heard from you in twenty-four hours."

"I can't get a damn signal on the cell here. But I've called. If you'd ever answer the phone, you'd know. Maybe I should have left an incriminating message on your machine last night. I'm riding with a ghost, Rod. You told me she'd have an accident. How'd you say it? 'I can handle the bitch.' You blew it and now I'm the one doing the goddamn work."

"The cab missed her. Should have taken care of it myself."

Brad snorted. "So, instead of her being in the hospital or dead, now all of a sudden she's the leader of the pack."

Rod ignored the jab. "The plan's changed. Just take care of both of them in California."

"You mean three."

"Three? Who else is there?"

"Dan."

"Dan? I thought the letter had scared him off." Rod paused. "This is perfect. You can take care of all three of them at once."

"Three? Why do I have to do all the dirty work?" Brad's gut twisted again. "I've got a bad feeling about this whole thing."

There was a hint of panic in Rod's voice. "Why? They onto something?"

Brad pulled a cigarette from his pack and lit it. "I think Jim can screw things up."

"I've told you, just keep your cool. We'll get through this, Brad. Let them get to California before you do anything. That'll give me time to get the plan together. Then it's over. Over! We'll split the money three ways and head for Mexico and tequila."

Brad impatiently ground out the cigarette after only a few drags. He lowered his voice to a rough whisper. "That's what you've been saying. Once we do this or that, it'll end. Once we send the letter, it'll end. Killing the dog was supposed to end it. Hit Alice and it'll end. Damn, Rod, don't be so... so arrogant. Things go wrong, like with the crash."

"I'm confident," Rod laughed. "Nothing wrong with that. Hey, neither one of us is in jail. Anything more?" He waited.

"Don't worry about me," Brad said as he hung up the phone and whispered "fuck you," not meant for Rod to hear. He headed back to his room.

Illinois

After Brad hung up, the man with headphones waited for the same click from Rod's phone. Upon hearing it, he recorded ten seconds of silence before turning off the tape.

He lifted the notepad. Had Rod actually told Brad to kill Alice, Jim and Dan in California? He rewound the tape and listened. "You can take care of all three of them at once." He fast-forwarded. "Let them get to California before you do anything."

The call had come from outside Sioux City, Iowa. Two days, maybe three, before they got to California.

Iowa

Jim exhaled frosted breaths as if smoking a cigar, trying to form smoke rings, and looked at Alice with each attempt.

"I want you to promise me something, Jim. We need to stay together until this is over."

He attempted one more smoke ring before answering. "Why? What's going to happen?"

"I don't know. It's a feeling."

Jim studied her, then tugged her hand to pull her closer. "Count on me. But what are you afraid of?"

Alice sat, shoulders hunched. "My dream. It's not the first. None of them ever make sense, but there's always this feeling of truth. Something about them is real. I hate it."

Jim nodded. "I know the feeling. Kind of real, but not. Flashbacks. I had them all the time in 'Nam. One time I..."

Alice interrupted. "A flashback. That describes it. But I never used drugs." She looked at him. "Except..."

His eyes opened wide, puzzled. "When?"

"After the crash, my leg broken. I was so drugged I barely remember any of it. Even when we met in Chicago, I was in a daze most of the time. Didn't you notice?"

He frowned. "Hey, who's the burn–out here? You or me? You think I was any better? I wasn't smiling all the time because I was happy." He lowered his head and kicked at the snow. "I needed every bit of it."

Alice moved closer and put her hand on his arm. "It must have been hell."

He looked up at the stars. "They never found Juliana after the crash." Reaching into the snow, he formed a ball and threw it with all his strength into the darkness. His arms dropped loosely to his side. "Months passed, Alice. Am

50

I a spaced-out idiot or what? I wanted her back in spite of the way she treated me. Every day, every knock on the door, every phone call, I thought it could be her. It didn't matter what had happened. I was ready to tell her *shhh*, don't talk. We're together again. That's all that matters." He blinked. "Now she's gone for good. I feel bad that weeks pass without thinking of her." He leaned back. "Tell me more about the dreams."

"Some have been me trying to get out of the plane just after it crashed. Some don't have anything to do with the crash. I'm in a car, it's hot, and the driver won't stop for water. Or I'm on a beach, crawling through the sand. It's rough and my knees are bleeding." She rubbed her knee to soothe the imagined pain.

He took both of her hands. "I know flashbacks, Alice, and they always have an element of truth twisted somewhere inside. We've just got to put our heads together and find it."

"In one dream I was in Chicago, on the plane, looking out the window before we took off."

"What did you see?"

"Can't be certain. What do we do now?"

"That's easy," Jim answered. "We go in."

"I need to be warm," Alice agreed.

They headed toward the light. Halfway to the door, she stopped. "I'm afraid, Jim."

He kissed her cheek. "We can look for caves if you want."

"I don't want to be alone."

Jim kissed her again. "I'm here."

Chapter Nine
PAPER AIRPLANES
Todd Possehl

Iowa

If one were to venture out from beneath the glare and artificial light of the Lucky 8 parking lot, and that one person were to look upward into the clear night sky, the faint luminescence of the Milky Way would show itself. And if that brave soul could endure the sting of a bitter February night just a few moments longer, a star would shoot across the sky. And yet even still, if the courage and patience of our amateur stargazer could hold out a little while longer, and he or she could not only look into the night sky, but listen, then the stillness would reveal how the light of the stars, the visible breath and the imagination are inextricably linked.

But no traveler on this night risked the darkness, the cold, or perhaps our story would have taken a different turn. So once again the artificial light won out over the true light. For the flesh is weak, and be it real or imagined, the flesh seeks comfort above all things.

Brad unlocked the door to a stale second-floor room, hung up his coat and placed all his valuables on a generic motel dresser top. He was careful not to make eye contact with his reflection in the large oblong mirror crowning the bureau, but at the same time congratulated himself on having the foresight to take a private room. The thought of sharing with either Jim or Dan would have been too much.

I don't know how much longer I can take this. I'll take care of business when the time is right. Screw Rod.

Brad felt a familiar stabbing pain in his stomach, sat on the edge of the twin bed closest to the door and doubled over. He needed release from the terrible secret and from what he planned to do. Looking deeper, he felt that something in his personality had been transformed, something beyond his grasp, as if some demon were re-creating him.

For diversion, Brad reached for the remote control on the nightstand. He noticed a flyer perched next to the remote and picked it up. Some First Baptist Church on Corncob Street was having a pancake breakfast, a three dollar donation asked. Brad laughed while creasing the notice several times, secretly envying the blue-haired Baptist women who had nothing more to worry about than half-assed church functions, and how high the corn crop was on July Fourth. He folded the flyer one more time, aimed just to the left of the large bureau and tossed a perfectly good breakfast towards a perfectly brown wastepaper basket. The paper plane looped once, hesitated and nose-dived into the hollow container.

Brad undressed, set the alarm for eight, chewed five Rolaids and hoped for a few hours of something more than fitful sleep.

"Dan will wonder where you are," Alice said as she stretched beneath the disheveled covers.

Jim sat up to put his boxer shorts on. "I wouldn't worry about him. I'm sure he's asleep."

Alice wanted to tell Jim how she felt, but didn't want to commit herself just yet, so she said, "Tell me about your poetry. How you came to read Blake."

"Got introduced to Blake in college, carried him around with me in 'Nam. That book was my Bible." Jim bent toward his JCPenney's bag and started rummaging around. He pulled out the book and extracted a joint from between its pages. "Found a writer's group when I moved to Nashville. Started writing some of my own."

"Been published?"

"'Apocalypse' made a local arts journal."

"How many people are in your writing group?"

"Oh, I don't go anymore. It's been years." Jim lit up.

"What happened?"

"The group starting writing this novel, each chapter was written by a different member, and like an idiot I volunteered to write the ninth chapter." Jim offered her a drag.

"No thanks. Then what?"

"The group wasn't fun after that. I mean I do poetry."

"What was the novel about?"

"Jeez, I can't remember, I think it was about some people taking a cross-country trip or something." They did a double take, looked at each other and laughed.

He coughed. "Alice?" Jim got serious. "About your dream. The reason I didn't blow it off is because I've had a dream too. A different dream. Recurring. I've had them ever since the crash and they're not flashbacks."

"Tell me."

"I'm driving along in my car and then something happens. It stalls, goes out of control, gets stuck. I get out of the car to look for help and notice that the whole world is crashing down. Trains derail; people flee for their lives; buildings going up in flames. Even emergency vehicles flip over."

"Wow, nice dream."

"Yeah, it's total chaos, and most of the time the dream ends with me running away from a falling airplane crashing down on me." Jim took one more toke. "But the last time I had the dream was the night you called to tell me about Charles, and the dream changed. At the end, when the plane was falling down on me, it suddenly turned into a paper airplane, circled gently above me several times, then landed softly on my lap."

"That's really bizarre."

"That's not all. I open up the paper plane and there's something written on it: ORDER CHAOS BECOMES, THE PRODUCT AND NOT THE SUM. And then lower on the page written in even bigger letters is: BUT IMAGINATION IS REAL."

Alice didn't answer.

"Well, what do you think?"

"Jim, come to bed. Come on, I'll rub your back."

"Reality. It's dreams, madness, gods and demons. It's all about mind and imagination. Blake knew. We create worlds on our own. There's no room for logic. I mean does anything make sense in this, in *this* world?"

"Don't WE?" Alice asked.

"It's all unreal—the crash, Charles—all made-up. The turboprop airplane is a paper airplane, right? That's all it is. Juliana's not dead."

"The pain I felt was real, Jim. The twisted metal, cold, heavy, sharp." Alice stared—tired and aggravated.

"No, I mean paper. It's all like written on paper. The airplane, you, me, Dan, everything. It's some story being written outside ourselves. You call this real? Then we exist in total absurdity. Don't you get it?"

"No! We need to go to sleep *now*, Jim."

Jim continued, "If I write a story about some chick drinking a few beers and dancing naked, then, in my mind at least, that chick really exists. She's buzzed, she's feeling sexy. I determine what happens next."

Alice turned over on her side, "You're high, Jim, goodnight."

Jim opened to a passage in Blake, a nightly devotional, or simply an old soldier's ritual to lull the fear of this life.

He leaned his head against the headboard and looked at Alice, her back turned toward him, "The Universal Baseball Association, Alice, you gotta read it. It's by Robert Coover. The characters come to life. The whole baseball league's on paper, but it's as real as Cubs versus Mets. It's all about the creative process." Jim sighed, and spent a minute studying his favorite poet before gently putting the fragile volume back into his bag. He picked up a flyer from the dresser top.

Alice wanted to sleep, dismiss Jim's version of reality, but she couldn't get out of her head the element of truth in what he was saying. Her dream alone forced her to question the nature of reality, and Jim had just realized the first part of that vision. This two-hundred-plus pound, burly, totally stoned Vietnam vet became her buffalo lover, and she was Jim's Juliana come back for the night.

Perhaps we do exist only in the mind, she thought. All that remains now is Charles. She would have to trust the "license allowed to poets" to write the rest of the story.

"It's two-fifteen, Jim. Turn out the light."

Jim obeyed this time.

"Alice?"

"What?"

"Do you like pancakes?"

Chapter Ten
CROSSING PATHS
Maryann Durland

Illinois

Jackson Opal crushed the lit cigarette under his boot into the snow and trudged around the block. He stopped at a trashcan jutting out of a snowdrift at a corner by a 7-Eleven. Cursing himself for buying them in the first place, he threw the Parliaments into the container. He felt stuck, much like the impact of the blizzard on the city. Chicago was buried. Airports were shut down, and most roads were clogged. Twenty inches of the white stuff was heaped on Cook County. Outlying suburbs had fared only slightly better with accumulations up to sixteen inches. Weather forecasters blamed Lake Michigan and what they termed lake-effect snow for the city's extra burden.

Jackson carried his own burdens written on his face; he knew even Opal's makeup couldn't cover them. All he could think about was Alice. Was she okay? Brad had slipped away with them. "That asshole," he said to no one but the frosty air.

California

"How's he doing?" Peter asked, standing in the hospital corridor. His voice was soft, his brown eyes sad. He spoke to the woman walking from room five-eighteen down the hall towards him. She was dressed in scrubs, her hair pulled back in a ponytail. Damp wisps of hair framing her face testified to the long, hot night.

"Looking forward to your visit." She paused a second, glanced back at the door, and then back at him. "The pain is a little less intense. He doesn't look quite so tired or so drawn this morning." She patted his arm. "Buzz me if we can get you anything."

He smiled. She walked away, but Peter waited in the hallway a few more seconds. He closed his eyes and leaned against the wall. For an instant he distanced himself from the past, the future, from every thought, every feeling. He placed himself only in the present, this moment. Nothing else clouded his mind. There was only today.

He opened his eyes, took a deep breath and walked down the hall to room five-eighteen.

Iowa

The sun was beginning to rise on a new morning as Dan took a map out of the car. He walked inside, sat in a rattan chair, and spread the map on the glass-topped coffee table before him. Dan traced a line with his finger and jotted notes on a hotel notepad. Jim walked over. "Blazing a new trail for us?"

Dan looked up. "Just checking our route. Get any sleep last night?"

"Slept like a baby."

California

Peter stared out the window. With his back to Charles, he gazed at the patients being wheeled along hospital paths. He knew every curve, brick and stone along the way. One year, all tied up in the details of a garden path. Each emotion and event symbolized by footsteps taken on those paths.

"Peter?"

He turned to look at Charles, so diminished in the chair. Peter saw the struggle in his eyes. "Can I get you anything? How are you doing?" Peter leaned toward his lover, touched his arm softly and added, "You look tired. Do you want to go back to bed?"

Charles shook his head. "I'll lie down in a little while." He sunk deeper into the overstuffed chair and reached for

Peter's hand. "I want to talk about our plans," he whispered. "I want to make sure that everything is okay."

"I'll do whatever you want."

Charles rested his head back, closed his eyes, and drifted off to sleep as Peter held his hand.

Iowa

Dan was surprised when Brad told him that he was renting a car and going off on his own, heading south towards Oklahoma and then on to California. Alice didn't care which direction he went; she was just relieved he was gone.

Dan, Alice and Jim had only been on the road a short time, still early in the morning, when the guys insisted that they pull over for breakfast. They stopped at that Baptist Church holding the fundraiser for a big breakfast of pancakes, sausage and coffee.

Back on the road, Alice gazed out the car window at the Iowa landscape. It was what it was: Iowa. She thought of how many versions of flat there were and how each could be so different. Even a level plane can still have a life of its own. Illinois's flat felt different from Oklahoma's flat. And this farmland's flat, even with the snow, had warmth.

Alice drew the letter *O* on the window and made a mental note to give Opal a call at the next stop. She turned to see Jim rifling in his Penney's bag.

Dan gripped the steering wheel. He needed to talk to Jim.

California

While Charles slept, Peter thought about the plane crash. Since making plans and sharing the details, Charles seemed more at peace.

Shortly after the crash, Charles had made a passenger list and compiled details that he could recall. It was his way to both remember it for the investigators and to expel the nightmares. They had written it all down. Peter typed as

Charles dictated, capturing the story of how Charles saved everyone.

But it didn't work. Visions and feelings popped up for months in dreams, flashbacks and sometimes in the middle of conversations. He continually relived that horrible night. Listening to Charles tell the story over and over, Peter knew almost as much about the crash as if he had been there. He knew about the letter and Charles's suspicions.

Peter also knew who had been saved; where they were in the plane; in what order each person was rescued; and what Charles had done to save each one. He hoped Dan and Jim and Alice would arrive soon. They had a lot to talk about.

Illinois/Iowa

"Alice?" Opal sounded worried.

"Yeah, it's me. Are you all right? We heard about Chicago on the radio, under an avalanche of snow."

"*Am I all right*? Yeah, sure. It's you, big Sista, that I'm worried about. How's that road trip going?" Opal held the phone close to her ear crushing an earring into the handset.

"Hey, everything's cool, and good news, we're moving at a decent clip. We missed most of that mess in Illinois, thank God. The roads were in pretty good shape in Iowa. And best of all, Mr. Brad's departed. And even better, I think I'm in love."

"Huh? Slow down, girl and give that to me again, one thing at a time. First, what's that about Brad?" said Opal reaching over to the CD player to turn the music off.

Alice unbuttoned her coat. It was warm, too warm inside the rest stop. "Yeah, Brad just up and took off on his own. I didn't even get to say good riddance. He told Dan early this morning, before I got up, that he was gonna split; we were traveling too slow for him."

Now it was Opal who was warm, slipping the baby-blue angora sweater off her shoulders. "What the fuck? Did he say anything else?"

"No, and frankly, I don't give a shit. He gives me the creeps."

"And that second thing you said, you used the *L word*. What's going on, Miss Sacagawea? What kind of expedition has Lewis and Clark got you on?"

"Opal, well I gotta tell you, this cross-country trip is bittersweet. It's a sad thing traveling to see a dying friend, but I think some good is also coming of this journey."

"Jimbo's got your big heart, huh?"

"Yeah... Hey, we gotta hit the road. But I'll call again soon. You go make a snow angel out there for me, okay?"

"And you keep the calls coming my way, promise?"

"Promise."

Nebraska

They stopped for a late lunch and got back on the road in less than an hour. Jim took a turn behind the wheel as Alice dozed in the backseat.

Dan glanced back at Alice still asleep. He could barely hear her breathing. "Jim?"

"Yeah."

"I think we need to talk about some things."

"Yeah, like what?"

"Well, I think we need to talk about, you know, things we haven't talked about. Important things I think we kind of know about, but don't really know the details about. You know," Dan said hedging and added, "Things."

"You're hemming and hawing like you're getting ready to tell me about the birds and the bees. If it helps, I've already had that discussion."

Dan laughed then cleared his throat. "No, Jim," he said turning serious again, "I mean things about the crash. What happened? What was going on? Those kind of things."

"Well, what is there to say? We all got a second chance."

"Something was going on. I really think so, Jim, but I don't know what. The letter we got. I know all of us got it, but we just did what it said to do. And why? What are we afraid of?"

"What did it tell us to do?"

Dan looked at him incredulously. "Didn't you get the letter?"

Jim took his eyes off the road for a moment and glanced at him. "Oh, I got it all right, but once I saw where it was heading, I threw it away."

"What?" Dan couldn't believe what he was hearing and at the same time it made perfect sense. "You mean, you never read the letter?"

"Yup, that's exactly what I mean. I didn't need to read that shit."

"Oh my God." Alice sat up and hit the back of Dan's seat. "That is the best thing I've heard in ages," she said laughing. "I wish I had thought of that. Instead, I got it, read it and freaked-out wondering who is doing what and why. We should have talked about this sooner. I could have done the same thing. He's smarter than us, Dan!"

California

After lunch, Peter helped Charles back into bed, again observing how frail his partner had become, ready to crumble away into fine dust to scatter over the earth.

When the doctor made her rounds, Charles asked to be released. She agreed and signed the discharge papers to permit him to go home the next day. Charles was relieved.

Eager to tell Alice the news, Charles asked Peter to call her, but he couldn't get through. He wondered if Alice, Jim and Dan would arrive in time.

Colorado

It was Alice's turn at the wheel. They decided to drive through the night, stopping only briefly to get gas.

Late in the evening, Alice called California and spoke to Peter. He told her that Charles would be home waiting for them, that he had things he wanted to tell them.

Chapter Eleven
TAKING CARE OF BUSINESS
Laurie Bohlke

Iowa

When Brad peeled out of the Alamo parking lot, the Jeep skidded on a patch of black ice and spun one-hundred-eighty degrees to face the steel spikes of the car rental exit. The gate was still lowering in front of the next car. Shuffling hurriedly out of his hut, the elderly attendant frowned at the car. Brad gave him the finger and backed the car around to start again.

"Screw you and your dead-end job," he muttered to himself. "Good thing I always carry that phony ID, just in case. I'm out of here—off to find those fucking idiots. Couldn't have gotten too far; they stop whenever someone sneezes. Moving way too slow for me. Couldn't stand wasting anymore time listening to them. Hope that skid's not an omen. Nah, I'm right to be doing this my way. No more taking orders from that asshole, Rod. Bet he'll be happy when I call with the good news. I'll just tell him my cell phone went dead. If I call him now, he'll try to talk me out of it. Better to off 'em here and now."

Brad sped past a small white church and didn't notice the unusual number of cars clustered around the church's entrance. Two pickup trucks sandwiched the '68 Buick, hidden from the road. Inside the church, Alice, Jim and Dan were wiping the maple syrup remains off their faces with thin paper napkins and heading for the door.

California

The hospital bed dominated the dining room—looming over the French-country china cabinet and its display of multicolored Murano glass fish. Jammed against the far blood-red wall, the mahogany table and damask chairs fought with the bed's stark-white sheets tucked tightly into its scarred metal frame. The Formica bedside table was ready—crowded with Charles's drugs, Kleenex in a ceramic container, a crystal alarm clock, phone and leather notepad.

The ambulance attendants strode into the room, bringing Charles's wasted body on a gurney. His labored breathing pierced the quiet. As they positioned Charles, sliding their blanket out from under his scrawny rump, the green oxygen tank thumped to the floor.

Peter hovered near the head of the bed, unconsciously steepling his fingers and tapping them together in time with Charles's breathing. Finally the paperwork was signed and the door shut. Charles and Peter were alone.

"What... what..."

Peter could barely hear him. He leaned over Charles, twisting his head to avoid the fetid odor of his breath. "What are you trying to say, Charles?"

"What... time..."

"What time will they arrive? Alice just called from outside Denver. They haven't even made it to Vail yet. It was forty and sunny when they passed the airport, but it was snowing hard by the time they reached Eisenhower Pass. They had to pull over at the next McDonalds to wait for the plow. Alice sounded damn impatient to get here and exhausted from driving straight through Nebraska last night.

"Do you remember when we skied Vail, Charles?" Peter's eyes glistened with unshed tears as he reached to stroke Charles's hand.

His skin ghostly white, his eyes closed, Charles sighed and his breathing stopped.

Peter gasped.

Then Charles's breathing began again, louder than ever. Peter paced back and forth in the small space between the bed and the table. This waiting was impossible. They just had to come in time.

Colorado

Back in the car, which reeked of leftover French fries, Dan girded himself to talk to Jim. "Jim, I've been trying to talk to you alone ever since Iowa. I don't want to freak-out Alice."

Jim interrupted, peering out through the flying snow. "How long is Alice going to take, damn it? Why do all women take so long in the can?"

"Just listen to me, Jim. There's something creepy about Brad. Weird. I saw him making a phone call from the lobby two nights ago. He was looking around like he was trying to hide from us. I don't trust him. Why did he come with us anyway?"

Suddenly the windshield exploded.

Dan slumped forward, blood splattering all over the front seat. Glass ripped into Jim's face. He reflexively ducked just before another bullet slammed into his seat.

Silence.

Wiping blood from his eyes, Jim cautiously raised his head just in time to see an amorphous shape running to a snow-covered SUV. It went skidding out onto the highway. War again. He absently tugged a diamond-shaped piece of glass out of his leather jacket right at the level of his heart. How many close calls in 'Nam? Bombs whining overhead. Mud, snakes, mines everywhere. So many friends dead. Pain…

Alice wrenched open the door that Jim was leaning against. She was out of breath. "Oh my God. Are you okay? I heard gunshots."

"What the fuck happened?" Jim asked.

Alice recoiled. "There's blood all over your face. Where were you hit? And…

"Dan? Dan!" She screamed as Jim moved enough for her to see Dan's still form slumped over the steering wheel. "Is he dead?"

Jim spoke slowly as he grabbed the scarf out of his Penney's bag to staunch the bleeding from Dan's chest. "Alice, Jesus. Call nine-one-one."

Adrenalin pumped and as Brad pounded the steering wheel. "Yes! I nailed one, if not two of them." He frowned. "Did I get 'em both? I gotta find out."

Jim recited "Tyger, Tyger" to himself as the ER doctor tied the knot on the last stitch closing the large cut over his eye. "Are you done?" he asked her, squinting at her nametag, Sylvia Lee, M.D.

Dr. Lee glanced across the instrument tray and shook her head. "Almost." She applied sterile gauze and tape, then removed her gloves. The nurse helped Jim sit up. Dr. Lee glanced toward a beckoning aide in the doorway. "Well, you're done here, Jim. Just keep this bandage dry for the next two days. No hair washing. I'm sorry that you had to wait so many hours. I'm sure you heard about the bad ten-car accident just west of here. We have a full house. Quite a number of injured people were admitted.

"At least we know that your friend, Dan, made it through surgery. There's a note here that your other friend, Alice, is on her way here from the police station."

Remembering what Dan had said right before the shooting, Jim said, "I've got to talk to Dan!"

"That's not possible now. He's in recovery. Just stay calm. We'll let you know when he gets a room."

California

Peter paced back and forth, back and forth. They hadn't called since yesterday, probably still debating over whether to stay with Dan in the hospital in Vail or head here without him. Hard to keep lying to Charles about the delay. Charles was so much worse and his lucid moments were infrequent. Peter had barely been able to rouse him to take his medicine at noon. Thank God the hospice nurse had gotten an order for a stronger pain pill when she visited earlier.

He couldn't pace anymore, collapsed into a dining room chair and closed his eyes.

Charles mumbled, "Juliana will pay." But Peter didn't hear.

A black snake slithered over the battered wreckage of the plane. Peter cautiously pushed aside the palm frond and peered into the darkened cockpit. He leapt back when a skull leered at him from the pilot's seat. I can't do this, he thought. Why did Charles tell me? He knows I'm not into rescue missions. I hate Harrison Ford films! Somebody else will have to figure this out. I'm going back.

As Peter turned away from the plane, a menacing rumble shook the ground. He fell to his knees as coconuts rained down around him. Monkeys screeched. The earth stilled. Rubbing his shoulder where a coconut had hit him, Peter stood up. What next? He stumbled toward a path winding between the trees, cursing fate. A soft rustling noise made him look up right into the greedy eyes of a salivating leopard that crouched, ready to pounce. Behind the leopard was Charles's ravaged body, blood everywhere. His dead eyes stared at Peter in reproach.

Peter jolted awake. Charles was awake, strangely alert. "Did you feel that earthquake, Peter? Our new alarm clock fell off the table and bounced off your shoulder. You're going to have quite a bruise."

Chapter Twelve
CHOICES
Joselle Kehoe

Chicago

Rod fidgeted with the polished chess pieces, rearranging the pawns on the black and white marble board on his desk. Game strategy was important to him. He squinted at the black king and its subjects as if the task required his sharpest focus. That king would never reach his white queen.

Lost in thought, he flashed back to a bar scene several months ago. He had drunk too much too fast and let down his guard. He attempted to entertain and seduce one of his female real estate cronies with stories about his exploits.

"You're a sick man, Rod," she had told him, and later commented that no sane person would expend such energy on that kind of useless manipulation.

But she underestimated Rod; most people did. The money was only part of his reward. This plane crash scheme was one of his most profitable endeavors, and it fascinated him with its complexity.

He smirked at the thought of those frightened mice, Jim, Dan, Alice and Charles meeting in his office last year. Their sober, investigative mood was laughable. God, that Charles was irritating, nobly dismissing all the praise and gratitude he received for his heroic rescues. As if that wasn't enough, he wanted to find the "truth." There had to be someone, something to blame.

Rod lifted a white pawn, rubbed it with his thumb, and said "Gotcha." Then he lifted a black pawn, squeezed it and added, "Brad, Brad, Brad, you son-of-a-bitch, where are you?" He was beginning to worry, but was far from reconsidering any of his plans. He knew Brad was losing patience, but he needed him to stay on track.

Rod noticed a speck of dust on one of the queens. He reached into the desk drawer for a soft yellow cloth and carefully rubbed each piece.

I wish I knew what Charles thought he was doing. I can't figure it out. What does he think he has to tell them? And why are the three musketeers on this pilgrimage to see him anyway? What's in it for them? I thought those assholes were scared shitless by my letter. Then they totally ignored my warning by starting on this trip. Hell, what am I worrying for? Brad will take care of them. But I've got to keep him under control. He can be such an idiot.

Rod knew it was a dangerous game he was playing. He'd become so good at creating problems where he was the solution. Things had gotten out of hand this time, but only marginally. As he stared down at the marble chess pieces on his desk, he contemplated his next move.

Colorado

Alice found Jim sitting in a treatment room. She stepped close and embraced him.

Jim shook his head and whispered, "What the fuck is going on, Alice?"

Alice leaned back. "The letter. It must be the letter. I can't believe this."

Jim eased off the exam table and reached for her hands. "We'll figure it out; we'll be okay. I just thought we were going to see Charles before he died, then all this shit started! I didn't believe the tape or care about the letter. All I care about now is you."

"Because Juliana is gone?" Alice asked.

"Juliana is gone, but her ghost is powerful," Jim answered.

"What's that supposed to mean? You're not making any sense."

"Why does everybody expect *life* to make sense? It never does! We create a lot of crap in our lives that we think we can't do anything about. But the crap we create is the only thing we can do something about. It's the truth. It's powerful, Alice, no matter what it looks like."

Alice stepped back, leaned against the wall, and let Jim rant.

"I'll tell you something," he said as he paced back and forth clenching his fists. "We can *say* what we think; we can *do* without money; we can *stash* a stupid letter if we want." His voice rose to a near shout. "We can stay stuck in time, or we can move on." He brought his face close to Alice's, and in a hushed tone said, "We can do whatever *we* want to do.

"I mourned the few good times I had with Juliana, the life I lived with her. I cried about the loss of what felt good—the dinners and soft clothes, soft chairs, cars that hugged the road—and the illusion we deserved it all; that everything was the way it was supposed to be. Yeah, everything was great on the surface, Alice, just great. You know what I mean? The truth is, inside there was nada, nothing, oblivion, indifference, death. I know I'm alive now. Juliana didn't care about me. She would have killed to protect her..." he hesitated for a moment looking for the word, "...her stuff," he finally said.

Alice was speechless. But, as she watched him resume his pacing, she felt grateful for his lack of refinement. She found his rough, unpredictable manner sexy but confusing. She needed to change the subject. "How's Dan?" she interrupted.

"At the moment, he's probably cruising around heaven."

"What!"

"No, no, you know, out of it, drugged, soothed to unconsciousness. I'm actually a little jealous."

She smiled, relieved.

Jim sat down and rubbed his brow as if he could rest his mind. "I'm so fucking tired. All I wanted to do was see Charles."

"We'll get there. First we need to see what the story is with Dan."

"He's probably the only one who can help us figure this out. I'm pretty sure about that now. Let's get some coffee or something and see if we can see him."

"You think he knows something?" asked Alice.

"I'm just pretty sure that he knows more than nothing, which is what we know." He thought for a moment, and then led Alice out of the emergency room. "Yeah, I can really see why they're trying to kill me," he said mockingly. "They're afraid I'll tell everyone about my flashbacks."

Chapter Thirteen
LET THE CARD FALL WHERE IT MAY
Bonnie Harm-Pechous

Colorado

The yellow light over Dan's bed competed with the soft blue glow of the moon on the snow outside the window. Jim sat in a chair and listened as Alice whispered into the phone, "Peter, that's awful! To dream that he'd died, and have it be so vivid. Is he that close then?"

Alice glanced at Jim, a look of concern in her tired eyes. Jim looked away, unable to bear her sadness. He'd never been good at confronting emotion. And now what? Dan is recovering from a gunshot wound. Charles is so close to death that his lover is having nightmares about it. It's just too damn much.

Alice hung up the phone. "So, are the cops done with us, or what?" She whispered, glancing at Dan and then the back of the cop guarding the doorway. "We've got to get to California; Peter says Charles doesn't have much time. But, how can we leave Dan?"

"One thing at a time, Alice. First, Dan's uncle's on his way here, so he'll take care of him. Dan would want us to get to Charles, that's for sure. As for the cops, they've got our home addresses; they have Charles's address and phone. They have a fucking file on us all. Long as we let them know where we're headed, they're fine. It's not us they want; it's the guy with the gun."

"Shit, shit, shit," Alice muttered, as she massaged her temples, eyes closed. "This has turned into a big, ugly mess, Jim. All I want to do is see Charles, is that too much to ask? Now this." She made a sweeping gesture with her hand. "Was this deliberate? Did someone mean to kill Dan? All that shit in the letter, it's coming true, isn't it? I'm done; I'm taking a flight out of here to San Francisco. We've got to get to Charles. We owe him that much. You with me or not?"

Jim sat looking at her. No, that's not what he wanted. He hadn't flown since the accident, but it looked like the only way to get to Charles now was by flying. "Okay, get on the horn and check the flights."

A movement outside the hospital room caught his eye. Just then the alarms started sounding from the machines around Dan's bed. Red lights flashed, nurses, doctors and a cop came running. Jim felt himself being pushed out of the way. He saw Alice by the door—eyes open wide—behind her he saw Brad. "What the hell!"

Alice turned to see what Jim was looking at but Brad disappeared. Jim moved away from the growing crowd of white coats and sapphire scrubs around Dan's bed. Everything was in slow motion, like the worst kind of flashback. Stomach churning, gut-wrenching memories flooded his mind. That's when he remembered the tarmac after the accident. He remembered watching the man searching the faces of the dead. That man was *Brad*.

"He's okay," the doctor said as Jim rushed for the hospital room door. He caught Alice's arm and headed after Brad.

"Jim, what's going on?"

"That was Brad!"

The snap of a door closing led them to a stairway right outside the surgical unit. Jim slowly opened the door and could hear the footsteps of someone running down the stairs. He motioned to Alice and they followed the sound.

"Oof!" Jim felt a fist slam into his face. Bright lights filled his darkened vision as he tried to keep himself from falling backward onto the stairs.

"Hey!" He heard Alice yell. He blinked away the darkness as he listened to Alice struggling with Brad.

Jim's vision cleared to see Brad's hands closing around her neck, her face turning purple-red. She scratched at his arms and swung at his face. Surging with anger, Jim jumped up from the stairs and grabbed Brad putting him into a headlock. He squeezed slowly and growled, "I've snapped more than a few necks in the woods of 'Nam. Dare me to snap yours?"

Brad struggled, but Jim's grasp on him only increased. Jim could feel Brad's breath shortening, his airway slowly being sealed. He made gagging sounds as he tried to breathe. He fought harder, grabbing at Jim's forearms, but Jim's strength was fueled by years of flashbacks, anger, fear and grief.

"Jim, stop! You're gonna kill him." Alice massaged her reddened throat, and pleaded again. "We need to know answers, Jim. We need him to talk and tell us what's going on. It's the only way it'll end."

Jim nodded. He lessened his grip and Brad fell to the floor gasping. Jim grabbed his collar and pulled him to his feet. "Alice," he said. "We're taking our friend for a ride."

The frozen rental car crackled as Jim, holding Brad's arms behind his back, shoved him in the backseat. "Alice, hand me your scarf." She pulled it off her neck and passed it to him. While Jim crawled in the backseat with Brad, Alice brushed the snow off the windows and then fired up the engine. Jim wound the scarf around Brad's hands, tying them behind him. "You're going nowhere."

Brad sat mute, eyes staring straight ahead. Jim sensed his fear, understood his fear, but didn't give a shit—the torture of the past two years, the deaths of Juliana and his parents, the nightmares, the anger—all of it an endless agony. In Brad's fear he saw an end.

He grabbed Brad's wallet and looked through it. "Hmm, one-hundred twenty-three bucks, driver's license. What's this?" He pulled out a business card and held it up to read in the glow of the parking lot lights—*Rod O'Neal?*

Brad looked at Jim.

"What?" Alice asked, seeing Jim's red face. He handed Alice the card in silence. "What does this mean?"

"How should I know? We need to get that information from our buddy here, but he's not talking, are you, asshole?"

Jim patted down Brad's coat pockets. "What's this?" he asked, pulling a blue-steel Smith & Wesson .38 caliber revolver from Brad's pocket.

"Oh God, Jim," Alice gasped.

Suddenly, Jim lunged into Brad, jamming his forearm across Brad's throat. "It's you! You're the fucker who shot Dan, aren't you. Why? You son of a bitch."

Jim pressed. "You gonna talk?" he growled.

"Jim!" Alice yelled, pulling on his shoulders. "Stop!"

Jim wrenched around and looked at Alice, his eyes dark and emotionless like a soldier's facing his enemy. "We need answers."

"If you kill him you'll go to jail."

"Alice, goddamit."

Jim relaxed his arm, and Brad rasped, "Okay, okay."

"Two questions, Brad. Why'd you shoot Dan, and what were you doing on the tarmac?"

A look of fear crossed the man's face, "What tarmac?"

Alice touched Jim's arm, "Jim, what are you talking about?"

"The tarmac, Brad. You were there, I remember. I saw you walking around the gurneys. Who were you looking for, Brad?" He asked, "Dan? Did you want Dan dead?"

"He sent me . . ." He nodded toward the front seat, his red face shiny from sweat.

"Who?"

"The card . . ."

"Rod? What the hell?"

"That's all I know."

"Shhh!" Jim hissed, as he leaned over Brad and peered out the window. "Security guard's coming." Moving fast, he flipped Alice the gun. "Keep him quiet."

He pushed open the door and got out of the car. Alice leveled the gun at Brad's head.

Jim fought the surge of adrenaline coursing through him as he walked toward the guard; his hands stuffed deep into his pockets. He had to be calm.

"Mr. Brill? Sorry to bother you," the security guard said. "You have a phone call. Said it was urgent."

"Oh, okay. Hold on a second." Jim walked over to the car and Alice opened the window a crack.

"Gotta go in for a phone call. Stay here, I'll be right back."

"What about him?" Alice whispered, hooking her finger toward Brad.

"He'll be okay for a few minutes, he's bound tight. I gotta get some answers and then we'll hand him over to the cops."

Alice looked at Jim and his eyes softened, "It'll be okay, Alice. Hold on for me. I'll be right back."

Jim sucked in his breath when the cold air hit him, moments later, as he walked out of the hospital again. He started to run, slipping and sliding on icy patches of the sidewalk, when he saw Alice standing outside the car door in the parking lot. She was rubbing the back of her neck and moving her head back and forth. The rear car door wide open.

"I don't know what happened," she said, her hands shaking. "I turned away for a second, then the next thing I know I'm lying across the seat. He hit me with something hard. Got a huge bump right here." She said, rubbing the base of her skull.

"Goddamit!" Jim ran around the car and down to the driveway of the parking lot looking for Brad. Nothing. Not a soul in the darkness. "Dammit!"

He saw Alice standing in the icy wind still rubbing the back of her head; he walked over to her and pulled her into his arms. "You okay?" he asked, smoothing her hair. Alice nodded into his chest.

"Son of a bitch got away. Do you still have the gun?"

Alice sighed, shaking her head no against him.

"Dammit."

They got into the car, and Jim retrieved Rod's card off of the front seat. "Okay, change of plans, huh?"

Alice shook her head. "What now?"

"We gotta tell the cops about Brad, about Rod O'Neil too. We'll call at the airport. We don't have much time—that was Peter on the phone." He held up the card to read it again in the parking lot lights.

"Hey," Alice said, as she pulled the card out of Jim's hand. "What's written on the back?"

Jim reached down and switched on the dome light. She turned over the card and gasped.

"What's it say?" Jim asked.

"I don't get it," she said, looking at Jim. "It says 'Juliana.'"

Chapter Fourteen
HEAVEN'S ROCK
Paul Cook

California

Jim and Alice spent the two flights mulling over the card.

"I still don't get it," Jim said. "I mean how many people are named Juliana? I've only known one and still regret it."

"Maybe it's just a coincidence," said Alice.

"Fat chance."

They spent the rest of the night at a small motel near Pismo Beach, south of San Luis Obispo. Sleepy-eyed, they had a late breakfast before heading to Charles's house. He was asleep when they got there, but it wasn't the Charles they remembered. He was pale and skeletal; his cheeks hollow, breathing with an oxygen mask.

"God," Alice whispered, shaking her head as she looked down at Charles's ashen face.

Jim nodded, "Yeah."

They stood beside Charles's bed until he woke with a start and focused on them. Alice rested her hand on his shoulder and Jim tried to smile. Charles fumbled with the oxygen mask and lifted it from his mouth, his breathing shallow. "You made it . . ." his eyes welled up. "Thanks . . ." Charles struggled to breathe. "Thanks for coming." Then he sighed and reached out for Peter's hand. "I'm so tired. I'm gonna rest now. We'll talk later. But go see my brother ... Peter will explain."

As Charles closed his eyes, Jim and Alice glanced at each other. Peter tucked a blanket around his shoulders, and then he motioned toward the kitchen.

"Brother?" Jim asked.

"Kirk is his brother; he'll tell you what you need to know. He's a minister at Heaven's Rock. It's not far from here," said Peter.

"Shouldn't we stay here?" asked Alice.

"No. Charles wants you to go now."

They followed Peter's penciled directions, driving the winding roads through sun-baked scrub, climbing the steep hills and following road signs until they reached the white gravel parking lot, surrounded by tall palm trees. When they stepped from the car, Jim tugged on his shirt to release it from the sticking dampness. He yawned and stretched, looking around. "Well, here we are," he said, then shrugged. "Where the hell are we?"

Across the parking lot, a man in khaki shirt and pants bent beneath the open hood of a blue Ford van. Metal against metal sounds echoed as he worked with a wrench. He straightened, rested the wrench on the fender and smiled as he walked toward them, wiping his hands with an orange cloth. He was muscular, in his fifties, with dull blond hair. His hands were rough and grimy, knuckles worn and bulging as if he had banged some heads together at one time or another, and he limped slightly. As he neared Alice and Jim, his facial scar became visible to them. It started high on his forehead, plunged down across his cheekbone, and tapered to a thin white line on his chin. Jim stared at the man. A knife fight? A broken beer bottle?

"Hi, you must be Charlie's friends," the man said, limping toward them and smiling. "He's told me all about you. How nice of you to come all this way. Please excuse my appearance. Been working on my van." He extended his hand in greeting. "I'm Charlie's older brother, Kirk." They shook hands awkwardly.

"Somehow we never knew about you," Alice said.

"Until an hour ago," added Jim.

"No. I suppose not. No particular reason you would. We all shared a house down in town before Charlie joined the airline. I've lived up here on the hill for twenty years." Kirk shuffled the gravel with the toe of his shoe. "I have two occupations. Insurance most of the time, and, of course, I moonlight as Pastor of the little church you see up there at the top."

He pointed upward to a redwood structure. "That's Heaven's Rock," Kirk said. "Charlie is a member here. When he dies, we'll have a simple service up there. That's his wish. I'm glad you came in time. Charlie's been so looking forward to seeing you." Kirk picked up a small stone and tossed it over the edge of the hill, watching it bounce down the slope. "The hospice nurse says it could be anytime now."

Alice and Jim were silent. "I notice you're staring at my scar," Kirk continued. "It's all right, everybody does. Fell on a pane of glass when our house caught fire some years ago. Broke my hip, too. Charlie saved my life. Ol' Charlie, always going around saving peoples' lives. Come on," Kirk said, moving across the gravel toward the van. "I'll drive you up and show you around. Too many steps to walk."

A huge boulder seemed to be growing out of the earth on one side of a redwood altar. It stood head-high to Kirk, much like half of a hard-boiled egg protruding from the ground. It was not smooth like an eggshell, but had all the ridges, curves and depressions that you might find on any boulder. Rows of redwood benches in a semi-circle formed the nucleus of the open-air church.

"When it rains," Kirk said, looking up at the clear sky, "it rains. I'm working on it." He smiled at his little joke. "And when I start rambling on at a service, which I frequently do, I can just half sit, half lean against the boulder and keep on talking while I rest." He patted the large stone, as if it were an old friend. "People ask if it has any religious significance. They want to think it does. I tell them it's just an ol' rock stickin' up out of the ground. They're always disappointed."

Alice and Jim sat down in the first row of pews. "It's beautiful up here, but we have no idea why Charles sent us to see you," Alice said.

Kirk leaned back on the boulder with his arms folded in front of his chest. "He sent you because I have a story to tell you. It's about the plane crash. By the way, Jim, let me ask you something. Do you like to fly?"

"Fly? Do I like to fly? Flying doesn't bother me too much if I've had about a gallon of Jim Beam in me and a cigar box full of tranquilizers in my backpack. Of course I feel safer all around if I'm sitting on the Pope's lap."

Kirk laughed. "You had a few belts the day of the crash, I'll bet."

"A few? Yeah, I had a few. My wife knew how I was about flying. She took good care of me. Always made sure I was well fortified."

"Your parents were on the plane when it crashed?"

Jim raised his eyebrows. "My parents? Yeah, why?"

"Did you know that the plane tickets for your parents were a gift from Juliana?"

Jim's eyes widened. "Why the hell does it matter who bought the tickets?"

"Please, let me finish. I have to tell you this, Jim. You're going to be angry. There was a lot of planning and plotting going on about this plane trip long before the crash, and a number of innocent people were murdered, including your parents. And here is the awful part—all courtesy of your wife, Juliana."

Jim stood up and looked hard at Kirk. "Listen, who do you..."

Alice put a restraining hand on Jim's arm. "Let's hear what Kirk has to say."

"I'm afraid it's true." Kirk paused. "And the motive behind all this, of course, was money—insurance and the inheritance from your parents. You changed your will, writing Juliana out after the crash, replacing her with Dan, Charles and Alice as beneficiaries. I've spent over a year of research on the crash. As I told you, my business is insurance. I'm an investigator. And, of course, I had a double incentive in this investigation because my own brother was almost killed on that flight. That's what happened. Your wife is a murderer."

"You're crazy! My wife was on the plane, sitting right next to me." Jim started to walk away. "I don't have to listen to this crap!"

Kirk raised his voice, "Was she, Jim? Or were you asleep? A little too much booze. A little drugged, perhaps, when the plane took off?"

Jim stopped and turned around to face Kirk. "Wait a minute, I don't get it. You're telling me ... my God ... Juliana killed my parents and herself?"

"Almost, Jim, but you haven't got it quite right." Kirk released a long breath. "I'm trying to tell you—Juliana is alive! Don't you see? She got off the plane. She's out there somewhere. And she still plans to kill you. That way everything goes to her."

"Oh my God!" Alice abruptly reached out for Jim. Jim's fists were clenched, but he remained silent.

"You realize you're still married? She's not been declared legally dead. They never found her body because there was no body to find. Believe me, she's got everything figured out, and can explain her long absence as some kind of shock or amnesia or something. She's very smart, Jim, very smart, but impatient. She'll make her move soon." Kirk shook his head. "Thou shalt not kill. But I'm afraid, Jim, that's exactly what she intends to do. Your wife, I'm sorry to say, is not a very nice woman."

Jim held Alice's hand tightly. "But how did it all . . ."

"Acid." Kirk paused, letting his words sink in. "We think she eased off the plane after you were too stoned to notice. As she did, she slipped a vial of sulfuric acid in the slots of the door hinges. Easy as pie. When they secured the door, the vial broke as it was suppose to, and the acid began to do its dirty work. Out over the water, the hinges popped just enough that the plane lost cabin pressure. Bingo. Blew the door off, but the plane almost made it safely back to land. *Almost.*

"That's what we think. That's what the FBI thinks too. Just last week they found the plane's door. Some fisherman."

Alice put her hand on Jim's knee, squeezing hard, as if transferring some sort of inner courage.

The ringing of a cell phone jolted them. Kirk fumbled in his pocket and put a small phone to his ear. He spoke briefly and then hung up. "Charlie's going."

A few days later, back at Heaven's Rock, several cars were parked on the white gravel. Mourners talked casually, milling together in small groups near the entrance of the church. The sky was a cloudless blue. Alice and Jim strolled around the edge of the parking lot, gazing down the hill and out at the ocean, shielding their eyes from the brilliant sunlight and thinking about all the days, all the months, and all the incredible events leading up to this moment—Charles's funeral.

"Look there," Alice said, pointing down the hill to several cars creating clouds of dust. "People coming up for the service, I guess."

"And over there," Jim pointed to a larger cloud of dust and several more cars coming up a different dirt road leading from the main highway. He pointed again, "Three limousines, for Chrissake." Within minutes the entire parking lot was filled with cars—some forced to park on the shoulders farther down the dirt road. Groups of three and four people struggled up the remaining distance on foot, perspiring, stumbling and turning their ankles in the ruts. Alice and Jim took their seats in the front row and waited.

Alice wished she were anywhere but here. She had always hated goodbyes—went back to her days in foster care, she knew. The mural behind the altar—blue mosaic behind the altar, decorated with flecks of glow-paint, representing the heavens—caught her attention. Alice found the Big Dipper, the Little Dipper, and the Milky Way. And then she made out the shape of a buffalo. Her eyes playing tricks, no doubt, but that's how it looked—the bison in her dream—with small stars spewing from its nostrils like puffs of fire.

In an instant of clarity, she realized that it had not been a bison in her dream that caused her orgasm—it was Jim, the thought of Jim. Jim was the buffalo of her dreams, the bison that rode between her legs. She squeezed Jim's hand, realizing that he had always been her dream. It had always been Jim.

The last to arrive was a gray-haired, heavy-set, veiled black woman. She struggled up the rutted road, her large, low-heeled shoes scratched and dusty, her heavy bosom shifting with each step. She removed an embroidered handkerchief from her leather purse and dabbed at the sweat running down her face.

She nodded to the lady standing next to her as she took her place in the back row. As she lustily sang the first hymn, *Amazing Grace,* she shifted her shoulders and dug at her bra straps. She scanned the audience and found Alice and Jim in the front row.

Kirk, wearing a navy blue, somewhat wrinkled blazer and khaki pants, limped his way through the crowd, greeting friends. He mounted the few steps leading to the rustic redwood altar and stood beside the boulder. The crowd became quiet. He cleared his throat and began. "I'll make it short," he said. "I guess you could say that this little church on top of the hill is a liberal church. Most of you sitting out there on those hard benches are pretty liberal folks—in your hearts and in your minds. Liberal thinkers.

"Of course, most of us came up here by taking different, and often twisting paths to get to the top, Heaven's Rock. Charlie was certainly one of those who took the hard way. Charlie's path was perhaps one of the most difficult—the roughest, toughest path of them all—the most excruciating. When Charlie was a kid, a teenager, his path became a maze, a jumble of confusion. He struggled mightily, and he suffered mightily. Oh, how he suffered. I know; I'm his brother.

"Charlie was gay. You all know that. It's no secret that he died of AIDS. But somehow, somewhere along the line, Charlie found a path that worked for him. It turned out to be a path of love—not of right or wrong, not of sin or no sin. Just a simple path of love. Charlie loved everybody, and today, love comes pouring back to him. Everyone here loved Charlie.

"There are two hundred thirty-seven men and women squeezed into our little church today. I know. I counted. Standing room only. From all over the country, from every town Charlie ever landed in while he was with the airline. The Mayor of our little town is here; my long-time friend, Judge Hobart, is here. And the rest of you, those without fancy titles, are here because of Charlie, love for Charlie."

Kirk blinked his eyes several times, and cleared his throat. "I don't want to become all weepy and sound corny. Charlie wouldn't want that. But I'm certain that somewhere, wherever it is, heaven's gate is swinging wide for him right this minute. And he is being welcomed with love. I'm absolutely certain of that. Charlie has friends in high places." Tears rolled down Kirk's face. "Well, I just want to thank you. Thank you all so much for coming to say goodbye to Charlie."

Scanning the crowd, the old lady noticed a man partially hidden by a redwood pillar, slowly reach inside his jacket. She squinted, looked closer and suddenly widened her eyes. It was Brad. Brad removing an automatic from his suit coat. For an instant, the old lady stopped breathing and then, in what seemed trained instinct, she fumbled inside her light jacket and jerked a revolver from a shoulder holster. In one motion she unlocked the safety and aimed the gun. The woman beside her let out a screech, throwing her hands in the air, her purse banging the revolver and knocking it into the air.

Brad jerked at the sudden sound and fired once, the bullet chewing into the wooden pew next to Jim. Jim threw his arms around Alice, slammed her to the ground and tried to push her beneath the pew.

As the old lady's gun hit the ground, another shot boomed, the slug careening off the boulder next to Kirk and burying itself in the mural. The mourners screamed; some dove to the ground.

Brad, pointing his gun wildly in all directions, ran out of the church. The old lady reached down for her revolver and ran after him, hobbling in her matronly shoes. As Brad slid down the hill on his backside toward the parking lot, the old lady followed, her dress pushed up, her butt scraping against stones and small cactus. The arm of a large cactus caught the lady's gray wig and pulled it off, revealing a sweating and determined Jackson Opal.

As they continued their long slide down the hill, they exchanged gun fire. None of the shots found their mark. Brad reached the parking lot first and dashed across the gravel to his car. He sped down the hill in a cloud of dust.

Jackson's falsies got tangled in a cactus, pulling the bulging pads from his dress.

Chapter Fifteen
DETOURS
Fran Fredricks

California

Jackson Opal brushed the dust off his dress after he stuffed the falsies in his purse and put the revolver back in its holster. Then he retrieved his wig, oblivious to the funeral attendees wide-eyeing him. Alice recognized her friend and ran over to him. Jim and Kirk followed.

"Jackson, my God! You okay?"

"No, Alice, I'm not okay. I let that idiot get away," said Jackson plopping the wig back on his head.

"Brad, that was Brad?" Alice questioned.

"Shit, yeah. Well, he shouldn't get too far. I've got back-up down the hill, but no time for chitchat, honey." Jackson turned to Kirk, "Better check on the mourners, Reverend, make sure everyone's all right."

Kirk nodded as Jackson ran, hips bouncing unnaturally, toward a car in the parking lot. Jim stood, slack-jawed, and watched him speed off, adding more dust to Brad's dust cloud that hadn't settled yet.

About thirty minutes later, the last limousine pulled away from Heaven's Rock leaving Jim and Alice alone. Jim leaned against the huge boulder near the redwood altar. As he stood there, he watched the car make its way down the hillside. "Alice, what the hell's going on?"

"I'm not sure." Alice walked to one of the empty benches and leaned against it.

Jim turned toward her. "Well, what's going on with Opal? What's with the get-up she, or should I say *he* had on? Playing Dirty Harry in drag? I'm confused."

"Jim, maybe I should have told you before, but Opal's a cross-dresser. I call her 'Opal' when she's dolled up, 'Jackson' when he's himself. He's my little foster brother. We grew up in Minnie's home together."

"I thought she, I mean he, was a fashion model."

"No," she sighed. "It's kind of like—don't ask don't tell. The clothing and wigs, it's just something she does. Never bothered me. It's a game really. But Jackson Opal's FBI. I didn't know he was on this case, but then he never tells me specifics. Confidential."

"Was he using us as bait?"

"No, no, never." Alice shook her head. "I can't believe that. He was here protecting us. That was obvious."

"So Jackson must know more than what Kirk told us. He must have been onto Brad all this time. And Brad must be Juliana's little thug, her hit man."

"Yeah. Now that I think about it, Jackson wasn't too happy about Brad hitching a ride out of Chicago with us. Even though we came close to being victims again, I feel pretty good knowing that Jackson is on this. I trust him with my life and yours."

They were silent for a few moments. Jim looked at the altar and bowed his head. "I should give a sermon. Tell everyone how not to live their lives." He folded his arms.

Alice sat on the bench. She smiled, her eyes sad. "Lovely place for a sermon. Kirk did a wonderful job with both the service and settling the crowd. Quickest and most exciting funeral I've ever been to. Wonder what Charles thought of it."

"I think his spirit was here saving me yet again. Jeeze, we almost had two funerals for the price of one. I feel like a cat who's lost count of what's left of his nine lives."

Jim traced an ancient crevice in the boulder with his thumbnail, smoothly, as a jeweler might cut a diamond. "Juliana is probably pointing a gun at me right now. Bang! She loves me. Bang! She loves me not. Bang! She gets my parent's money." He looked at Alice. "Come over here by me."

Alice shook her head and smiled. "And get shot at?" She stood anyway, then quickly sat down. "I forgot you're a married man."

Jim sighed heaving his broad shoulders. "Can you believe it? She planned to kill my parents and me and then take off with the inheritance. I never think about money. I guess that's all she thought about. There was a time I thought it was me she wanted."

Alice walked to his side. "I didn't know your parents had money," she said. "And I want you."

"Let's get outta here, Jim, before cops come questioning again." She paused and watched as Jim turned his attention to the boulder. "You know I have to be going back to Oklahoma. Work calls. I want life to return to some semblance of normalcy. Come with me."

He hugged her. "And I want you. I want to go with you, Alice, but I'm afraid I'll put you in danger."

Alice looked up at the blue mural buffalo again. "I just want to be with you."

"When do you want to leave?"

At the airport terminal, Jackson Opal dialed his bank, punched in his PIN number and selected number four from the verbal list of options. A voice confirmed his selection.

"You have selected checkbook balance. If this is correct, press pound."

Jackson pressed pound.

"Your balance is twenty-four dollars and five cents."

Damn, he thought. The government's getting slower every month. He pressed a button located on the bottom of his phone and redialed. Again a mechanical voice answered. "Federal Bureau of Investigation."

He spoke carefully. "Extension four-five-nine-three." After several beeps, a connection was made.

"Jackson, you son of a gun. Last time you called was to complain about your check."

"Déjà vu!"

"What? They screwed up again?"

"Did Hoover wear panty hose? Of course they screwed up! Would you take care of it? I'm getting low. Remind them it's called automatic deposit for a reason."

"I'll tell them. Anything new?"

"Yes, our main perp got away. I'm ordered back to Chicago in the middle of all this. Of course I can't get a direct flight; have to go from San Luis Obispo County Airport to LAX first. And I've lost track of Alice."

"So what's the coverage then?"

"Agents are on alert from here to the Mississippi, but I'd still rather be on this end of the case. Shit, I fucked up, so it's back to Chi town for me, and no time for the crying game. Hey, I gotta go, got a flight to catch. Now don't forget about my money."

"You can trust me, Jackson. I'm like you. I work for the government. And hey, don't be so hard on yourself. We all fuck up. It's part of this gig."

Nevada

The billboard read, "Welcome to Fabulous Las Vegas, Nevada." Alice lightened her foot on the gas pedal and took another chug from the can of soda she retrieved from the cup holder. Jim shifted in the passenger seat. "Alice, let's stop in Glitter Gulch, find us a wedding chapel and get hitched. We can have our reception at one of those all-you-can-eat prime rib buffets. Have us an overnight honeymoon and hit the road in the morning."

"You're not serious or delirious are you?"

"If others had not been foolish, we should be so."

"You're quoting Blake again. Hmm, okay, it's delirium. Crossing the desert will do that."

"Alice, Alice. I just love you. Besides, he who desires but acts not, breeds pestilence."

"Sounds like Blake didn't know about bigamy."

"Oh yeah, I keep forgetting. I want to forget for now and just enjoy you," he said and ran his fingers through her hair. Alice glanced at him and smiled.

"Oh, here's some worthy Blake, perfect for the moment," Jim said as he rifled though his JCPenney's bag and retrieved his tattered book:

I went to the Garden of Love,
And saw what I never had seen:
A Chapel was built in the midst,
Where I used to play on the green.

And the gates of this Chapel were shut,
And Thou shalt not writ over the door;
So I turn'd to the Garden of Love,
That so many sweet flowers bore,

And I saw it was filled with graves,
And tomb-stones where flowers should be:
And Priests in black gowns,
Were walking their rounds,
And binding with briars,
My joys & desires.

 Jim closed the book and put it back in the bag. Alice reached over and squeezed his hand. "Yes, let's pretend, for a little while, we've no cares in the world. There's only me and you and a buffet calling."

 The Nevada Palace was the first hotel Jim and Alice pulled into off Boulder Highway. It was kind on the wallet with an available room. They registered. Tired from the road, full from a meal, both wanted a shower and a bed to crawl into.
 "That San Remo prime rib was really pretty good," said Jim slipping the room key into the lock. "And at four-ninety-five, it was a good deal, too."
 "I agree. My filet was done to perfection, and I also think we sound like a commercial. But thoughts get lazy and conversation gets simplistic, mundane when you're tired. I'm tired," said Alice following Jim into the hotel room. The lingering smell of smoke, Dial soap and Pine-Sol surrounded them as they kicked their shoes off.
 "I should take a shower, but all I want to do is get under the sheets and make love to you right now. I'm impatient for you," Jim said putting his arms around Alice. He started kissing her neck. "You taste good."
 "You feel good," Alice said slowly moving Jim toward the bed. She pulled at his shirt while he started undoing her blouse.
 Jim took his time gently working down the line of buttons. And as he pushed each one through its button hole, he whispered, "If you trap the moment before it's ripe." He

moved to the second button. "The tears of repentance you'll certainly wipe." The third button. "But if once you let the ripe moments go." The last. "You can never wipe off the tears of woe." Blouse open, he brushed it off her soft shoulders, letting it fall to the floor.

He pulled his hands away momentarily and looked at her. "You are beautiful." Then he reached for her and they tumbled on top of the bed. Alice kissed his eyelids, his cheeks, his nose and chin, and then pressed her open mouth to his greedy lips. They rolled over the rumpled bedspread, squirming out of their remaining clothes.

Legs entwined, they held each other the night through as if the last coin had been dropped, the topless dancers had covered up and gone home, and the bright lights of the Strip had been switched off. Nothing outside motel walls existed for sleeping lovers.

Chicago

The answering machine blinked with seven messages. Jackson Opal listened intently. The only ones worthy of his time were from FBI headquarters and from Alice.

One gave orders to fly out to Oklahoma immediately. Another chance for a showdown was just what he wanted to hear. But Alice's message about going home came with mixed reaction.

"Hey, Opal. Sorry we didn't stick around for the investigators, if there were any. Jim and I just weren't up for it. I don't think we could have offered any useful information, anything you didn't already know about. Shit, you know more than we do. I wish you had told me you were on this case. Anyhow, we are on the road home. I'll call again soon. By the way, I loved the old lady look."

Jackson tried to call Alice back on her cell phone, but no one answered.

"Damn, Alice. Don't go home. Not now," he said to himself as he dialed his office at O'Hare Airport. When the connection went through, he told the secretary he would not be coming in, other duties called. "Don't schedule me for a while. It's not hooky I'm playing at, it's official business taking me away again." Then he called United Airlines and booked a flight to Oklahoma.

Unbeknownst to Jackson Opal, another set of tickets was booked for the same flight.

Chapter Sixteen
IN FLIGHT
Joe Hebert

Chicago

There were no flights available to Oklahoma until the next morning. Jackson thought it wiser to travel as Opal. He didn't want to take the chance of anyone recognizing him at the airport and catching him in his little lie. Any excuse to dress as Opal worked for him.

Jackson spent the evening at home modeling different outfits and decided on a red blouse with fitted sleeves, a black-velvet skirt with a slit up the side, and a paisley silk-scarf loosely tied around his neck to hide his Adam's apple. Jackson, admiring his profile as he smoothed his blouse and adjusted his falsies, "Oh, you are so damn sexy, Opal, too sexy for your clothes! Hoover had nothing on you."

Satisfied with his choice in wardrobe, Jackson packed his suitcase while his mind focused on more serious matters.

Juliana was just twenty minutes away via the Ravenswood "L." She felt at home living in the city. Chicago, just like the old song, was her kind of town. The hustle and bustle made her feel alive, not like the drab existence she had with Jim in that god-awful backward town in Tennessee.

Juliana was a petite woman of five-foot-four, but not as petite up top as she had been before the crash. Rod had paid for her breast enhancement along with a slight touch-up on her nose. Her hair was now blonde, not auburn, and she wore it shoulder length. She sat at her dressing table and applied sheer eye shadow to offset her green eyes, and smiled approvingly at herself with bright, bleached teeth in the mirror as she brushed on black mascara. There was no denying her outer beauty.

Juliana wasn't going to spend the night alone. She rarely spent the night alone. It didn't matter who or where, it was the conquest that excited her. Men were to be used and she was good at it.

She wasn't going to live her life catering to someone else anymore. She had played Jim's "angel" when he came back from 'Nam. Jim had everything Juliana ever wanted. He was handsome and kind, with money and all the right equipment. However, all that seemed to matter to him was reading poetry and living in a fantasy world. Jim never cared about his money and ever since the day he came home to find Juliana riding the neighbor on their kitchen table, Jim had cut her off. No sex, no fun, no money. Bastard. Jim's going to pay, Juliana thought. Yes, he's going to pay.

The phone rang five times before Juliana picked up.

"Hi, it's Rod."

"What's up?"

"Join me for dinner tonight."

"Nope, I'm just getting ready to leave."

"Where to?"

"Out."

"We're flying out tomorrow, you know."

"Yeah, I know. I'll be there."

"I thought we were going to spend the evening together."

"You thought wrong. Bye." Juliana hung up the phone, checked herself in the mirror one last time and left her building to hail a taxi.

Pork Chops—Juliana's favorite testosterone hunting ground. It was a renovated warehouse, a massive nightclub where the dance floor and the bar are separated by two castle-sized doors. She found an empty spot at the bar and was greeted by one of the bartenders. "What can I get you, honey?"

"Gin Martini, two olives."

She pulled out a compact from her purse to check herself one more time. Satisfied, she snapped the mirror closed and placed it back in her purse. A young man, nearly half her age, squeezed in and sat next to her. He extended his hand. "Name's Bill. Can I buy you a drink?"

"Juliana. Sure." They had several drinks as a companion to their meaningless conversation. Sucking on an olive, Juliana leaned into Bill, "Touch my arm."

Bill obliged, "Mmmm, soft."

Juliana whispered in Bill's ear, "That's what my ass feels like."

"Is that right?" Bill asked, as he reached around to grab her behind. Suddenly, a paper airplane landed on the bar. Juliana turned and looked behind her.

"Not funny, Rod."

"I knew I would find you here. Let's go."

"I'm not going anywhere."

Bill interjected, "Excuse me! The lady and I were having a conversation."

"Listen pal. This ain't no lady and your conversation is over."

"Say's who?"

"Don't give me no macho bullshit." Bill stood up, towering over Rod, and without hesitation punched him in the face.

Juliana drove Rod's Jaguar back to her apartment. Rod pulled down the vanity mirror to look at his swollen eye.

"I wish I never saw you get off that plane. You're nothing but trouble."

Juliana laughed. "You like trouble, Rod. *And* you love my new tits."

"Like I said, why did I ever get mixed up with you?"

Juliana parked the Jag in front of her building and turned the keys over to the valet attendant. They rode the elevator to the twelfth floor in silence. She unlocked the front door, flipped the switch in the hallway, and Rod followed her in.

He plopped down on the couch. "I don't know what I'm doing here. I've had enough for one evening."

Juliana kneeled in front of Rod and unzipped his pants. "Let me make it up to you."

New Mexico

Jim and Alice continued driving through the night on their way to Oklahoma. Their journey had become longer than either of them expected. "Do you realize how lucky we are, Jim? We've survived a plane crash and a couple of bullets that were meant for you."

Jim just shook his head. "Incredible."

Alice placed her hand on Jim's thigh, letting her fingers slide higher. Jim took his right hand off the steering wheel and squeezed Alice's hand.

"Jim?"

"What?"

"What else have you got in the Penney's bag?"

"Nothing, just personal stuff."

"Like what?"

"You know. Some poetry I've written. It's no big deal."

"Can I read some?"

Jim shook his head. "I'm no Blake."

Alice reached into the Penney's bag, pulled out a tattered notebook, flipped through it and found a poem scribbled in tiny black letters. She read silently a moment and then read aloud:

Home
The trees green and lush
The sky blue and clear
Yet I lay here in fear

Fear that this will be
My last day here
And so I wait.

Wait to see
If I will be found
I hide beneath my brother

My brother is stabbed
With a bayonet
Doesn't matter he's already dead

Dead and so are thousands more
The hunted hunt and roam
Will I ever make it home?

Chicago

Rod and Juliana, seated in first class, ordered Bloody Marys for breakfast, double shots. Rod wore dark sunglasses to hide his black eye. Juliana stirred her drink with a celery stick and Rod meticulously folded his napkin into a paper airplane. "You know I hate when you do that, Rod. What the hell's your problem?"

Rod just laughed and launched his napkin at Juliana.

"Final call for flight one-five-eight-seven to Oklahoma City. All rows boarding."

Opal Jackson was out of breath when she handed her boarding pass to the flight attendant.

"Row twenty-seven-C."

Opal entered the aircraft and made her way toward the back of the plane. Rod couldn't help but notice the tall dark-skinned beauty make her entrance. As Opal passed by, Rod turned toward the soft scent of Chanel No. 5. He tilted his head, peered over his sunglasses and whispered under his breath, "Nice legs!"

Chapter Seventeen
BY THE TIME I GET TO TULSA
Nancy Wedemeyer

Arizona—Texas

Outside Kingman, Jim and Alice picked up Interstate 40 that would take them into Oklahoma City. From there it would be less than two hours to Tulsa and Alice's apartment. They were both weary of white lines, highway signs and blurred landscapes viewed at seventy-miles-per hour. Alice longed for a hot soak in the tub, and Jim needed some time alone with Blake.

Near Amarillo, Alice peered out the window at the rain clouds gathering to the north. Involuntarily she shivered and stared at Jim's profile, eyes fixed on the road, forehead creased in concentration. She opened her mouth, hesitated, uncertain if the time was right and if Jim was ready. So many ifs, yet there was so much they needed to talk about. Touching his arm, she tried again.

"Jim, why Juliana? From what Kirk said and what you've told me, she doesn't seem like the type of woman you'd ever fall in love with. I don't understand."

Jim looked over at Alice, then returned his gaze forward. He sat as still as stone, forehead creased deeper, chiseled, while his hands gripped the steering wheel.

"I've been thinking about that for the last year. First I had to wrestle with the guilt of her death, and now I find out she's alive. She killed my parents and tried to kill me." He looked ahead at the sky and said, "*'Though those that are betrayed/Do feel the treason sharply, yet the traitor/Stands in worse case of woe.'*"

"Blake?"

"Shakespeare."

"And?"

"I don't know if I have the answer. I know I was lonely after 'Nam, a little freaked-out, and she was a warm body in bed at night. But the sex fades and you need something more to build your life on. She realized the same thing about the same time, and started acting on her fantasies while I withdrew into mine. Our marriage limped along for years as we led our separate lives."

"But you were going on vacation together?"

"A last attempt to fix us. I don't think either one of us thought we had a chance, but we needed to try. Even Juliana. She wasn't always as terrible as the things she's done." Jim's body language signaled an end to the conversation and they lapsed into silence for the next ten miles.

A few drops of rain hit the windshield, a few more, then lightning streaked the sky, answered by a booming thunderclap. Alice jumped. Storms scared her, but she kept her fear under wraps when flying. On the ground she sometimes gave into her panic, remembering nights huddled with Jackson in the bedroom closet at Minnie Owlfeather's. The wind picked up speed, buffeting the car between the lines, adding another layer to her fear. Shaking, Alice ducked her head, stuck her face near the windshield and looked up. Still very dark. They must be right in the middle of it. She knew Texas storms could pass rapidly, but they could also devastate quickly.

"Are we near a town?" she asked.

"You sound funny, Alice. Are you okay?"

"I don't like thunderstorms. Let's stop for coffee someplace that's more protected than this piece of metal."

"It's heading south. We'll drive out of it in a few minutes."

"Now, Jim."

Three down-at-the-heel houses and a combination gas station-diner appeared a quarter mile ahead. Jim turned into the parking lot, pulled next to the concrete block building. Alice scrambled out, running for the door before Jim put the car in park. A blue sedan cruised slowly past the diner, pulled off the road onto the shoulder and shut off the headlights. The driver turned and looked over the backseat toward the building.

Standing inside, water dripping on the tile, Alice scanned the near-empty room and hurried to a booth at the back, away from the windows. Jim walked in and shook himself like a freshly washed dog before joining her. He sprawled in the seat across from Alice and smiled. "Alice, you're brave enough to hang out with me and take a chance on getting shot, but afraid of a little old panhandle storm. It's good to see there's still something that can shake you up."

Thirty minutes later they were once again heading east. The air shimmered with color from moist reflections of the afternoon sun. The blue sedan tore by them, driver focused on the road, baseball cap pulled low on his forehead.

"Check out that guy," said Jim. Musta been going close to a hundred."

Chicago—Tulsa

Opal glanced at her admirer as she struggled in the aisle with her carry-on, ankles turning from the heels she wore. She took a second glance at the back of the dark-haired man, sensing a familiarity, but unable to identify him from behind. The blonde woman sitting beside him also looked familiar. When she reached her row, Opal hoisted her bag up to the overhead compartment, wedging it between a duffel bag and hard-shell attaché case. She stashed her laptop under the seat in front of her.

Opal sat next to a little boy and his mother. The child, who looked about five-years-old, was dressed as Superman, complete with cape. As he sucked on something sticky, little drops of goo occasionally dripped from his mouth. Thinking about her beautiful skirt, and silk Chanel blouse, Opal shifted her body toward the aisle. Come near me kid and I'll break your little fingers, she thought, smiling in the general direction of the mother. This wouldn't happen in first class.

She could feel the boy's curious eyes on her, looking from her well-coifed wig to her tired feet like he had X-ray vision. She wouldn't look at him, though. No need to encourage his sticky interest. She eased her aching feet out of the black pumps, and wished she'd worn different shoes. These new shoes squeezed her feet like a vise. She rubbed one stocking covered foot over the arch of the other and then reversed. As Opal buckled the seat belt, the captain's voice came over the intercom and announced their departure.

"Billy, quit staring at the nice lady." Billy's mother turned to Opal. "Hi, I'm Kathryn Wilson. We're on our way to Grandma and Grandpa's house. It's Billy's first flight."

"Hello, I'm Opal Jackson," she said pleasantly, flipping open the new Vogue she bought at the airport newsstand. A fold-out section on a line of Italian leather coats caught her eye, and she focused on the page until a small voice grabbed her attention.

"You've got really big feet," said Billy, leaning over to stare at Opal's unshod appendages.

"Billy!" said Kathryn, pulling him up by his cape. "Sorry about that."

"No problem," Opal said, glaring at Billy after Kathryn once again focused her attention on the window.

The plane accelerated, racing down the runway. With an engine surge and swoosh, it lifted from the ground, forcing little Billy against the back of his seat. He remained quiet for two minutes then resumed chattering to his mother.

Opal got up and walked toward first class looking for a flight attendant to check availability of other seats. She didn't see any open seating in coach, but maybe she could upgrade. A quiet conversation with one of the attendants, a few minutes wait, and Opal took a seat up front, across the aisle from the couple she noticed upon boarding.

Attempting to hide her interest, Opal stole glances at the man and his blonde companion. It had to be him. She snagged her laptop from under the seat and logged on to the FBI database, pulled up her files and found the one she was looking for. It was an FAA investigation file from the crash Alice was in. Scrolling through several pages, Opal opened the one that contained photographs of the six survivors. She tilted the laptop away from the aisle, toward the empty seat next to her, and examined the images. Yes, yes, yes. The man in the photograph, sans sunglasses, was Rod O'Neal.

She opened another file, the one of those missing and dead from the same crash. Fifteen faces appeared on the screen. Opal took a second look at the photo of an auburn haired, attractive woman, with a hard look to her green eyes—Juliana Brill. As she leaned forward in her seat, Opal pretended to drop a pen and picked it up while scrutinizing the blonde across the aisle. Pay dirt. Juliana, with a different hair color. What were these two doing together? It was time to meet her flying companions.

Opal slipped her watch from her wrist, dropped it in her purse and leaned into the aisle looking at Rod. "Excuse me, do you know the time?"

Rod looked her up and down with his own version of X-ray vision, and responded, "Yeah, it's a little after one Chicago time."

"Thanks. My name is Opal, Opal Jackson," without extending her hand.

"Rod, and this is Ju ... uh ... June." Juliana's look launched missiles to Rod's head. He was staring at Opal and missed the incoming weapons.

Opal continued, "I've never been to Tulsa before. Do you know a good hotel there?"

"The Adams Mar—" Juliana spiked Rod in the ankle with the tip of her shoe, and he turned briefly away from the attractive woman across the aisle. "Or the Hilton's good, too."

Opal noticed the foot shot and decided to back off.

"Well, thanks. I just might try one of those." She picked up her Vogue and thumbed the pages, keeping her ears open to conversation. But her new traveling buddies whispered in furious undertones too quiet to discern the words.

The flight ended in sunny Tulsa at two p.m. Opal gathered her bag and computer and followed Rod and Juliana off the plane into the terminal. She lagged behind, pretended to make a cell phone call and watched to see if they'd head to the luggage carousel. No. Apparently they were traveling with carry-on only.

Opal watched them head to the taxis waiting outside. She smiled in a distracted way and waved goodbye to the couple as she climbed into a cab of her own. Still smiling, she looked at the driver, a heavy-set, forty-something man. "You ever follow anyone?" asked Opal.

"Not my business. I drive cabs."

"There's an extra fifty for you if you keep up with the taxi that's pulling out now. It might be heading to the Adams Mark Hotel."

The driver studied Opal's face, turned back to the front and sped away from the curb, keeping the other cab in sight.

The registration line was short, and Opal stood behind Rod and Juliana. After exchanging brief hellos, she looked at the lobby, pretended distraction and listened carefully to the couple's room assignment. Sixth floor. When it was her turn, she asked to see a floor plan, then asked for room 619 stating they were her lucky numbers.

"I'll see if that's available," said the clerk. Apparently he wasn't alerted to anything unusual about Opal's request. He'd probably seen it all.

The room, across the hall and three doors down from O'Neal and Brill, was medium-sized with a small, mirrored entry hall. Opal left the door cracked and sat on the bed to watch the hallway in the mirror. Anyone on this floor would have to go by 619 to get to the elevators or the stairs. She kicked off her shoes, grabbed the phone and called the Chicago office. After filling them in on her discovery, she hung up and waited for a call from Agent Grey, her contact in Tulsa.

While watching the doorway, she removed her makeup and changed clothes, donning a man's suit. He wasn't going as Opal to the next encounter. After strapping his holster under the suit coat, he checked his weapon and was once again Jackson Opal, FBI agent.

A blue sedan cruised in front of the brick, two-story apartment building at 311 S. Owasso Street and parked along the curb a block further south as the driver scanned the neighborhood. Brad got out removing his baseball cap. He strolled at a leisurely pace up the block and looked at the door buzzers. Pressing a button for "Baskin" on the fourth floor, he waited for a response. When none came, he tried a different buzzer.

"Yeah?"

"Flowers for Baskin."

"They're in four-two-four. You've got four-one-four."

"I know. There's no answer and I need to leave these with someone. Will you accept delivery?"

The door buzzed, muffling "Yeah, okay." Brad sprinted up to the second floor and found apartment 212. Using a well-worn set of picklocks, he made short work of the flimsy barrier and was inside in seconds. The apartment smelled unoccupied and musty. The drapes were drawn against the afternoon light. Determined, Brad hurried down the hallway. He rejected the master bedroom, and turned into the second room. It held a wooden desk, rolling armchair, and daybed dressed in Indian blankets pushed against the wall. He opened the closet door and looked over the interior. Yeah, this would do. Enough clothes to hide behind and enough room to be comfortable while waiting. The closet shared a wall with the living room; he'd be able to hear them come in. Grabbing two pillows from the closet shelf, he threw them on the floor, stretched out on their softness and closed his eyes for a quick nap.

Chapter Eighteen
A LITTLE GRILLED CHEESE IS A DANGEROUS THING
Elliott Sturm

Tulsa

Alfredo Tapia was in a very bad mood on the last morning of his life. He woke up in the back of his old black van, sick drunk from the night before, and still pissed that his wife had refused to let him in the house.

"Bitch don' know how good she got it wit' me," he mumbled as he lay on his back, trying to stop his head from spinning.

Lupe, Alfredo's wife, was a patient woman. She had been patient with him for seventeen years. She had been patient when he stabbed a man in a bar over another woman. She had been patient with him when he came home drunk the last ten thousand times. Now she was done. There was no more patience in her. She stood in the living room of their old brick bungalow and happily stirred her thick, sweet coffee and looked through her front window, watching the pigeons clucking around her front stoop. His black van was still in front of the house, and she knew he was in it, but she didn't care.

Inside the van, Alfredo sat up too quickly and the nausea hit him. He puked on his knees.

Alfredo's life was usually ruled by two emotions—anger and resentment. This morning, those two old friends held him close, reluctant to let go. He wiped himself off with a crusty towel and climbed over to the driver's seat. He looked around blearily and tried to think of where to get a drink. He pulled down the sun visor and grabbed a small brown vial with a little bit of white powder left in it.

"Hey, it's the breakfast of champions," he said as he tilted his head back and inhaled the last of the coke. He tried to look into the house to see if Lupe was sitting there laughing at him. He knew if he saw her laughing, he would kick down the door and break her neck with his hands, but he couldn't see though the reflections in the window. It was a good morning for Lupe.

Alfredo started the van and the old motor belched out smoke for a couple of minutes until it warmed up. He put it in reverse and banged into the car behind him. "Asshole shouldn'a parked so close to me," he said. He put it in drive and headed down the street for a couple of blocks, wiping his mouth with the back of his hand. He tried to shake his head clear, but it only made his dizziness worse. He reached for the radio to turn it on, but as he leaned forward, he pushed the accelerator to the floor. His body flew against the back of the seat. Confused now, he pushed the gas pedal harder, thinking it was the brake. He tried to get control, but it was too late. The needle of the old speedometer passed sixty-five miles-per-hour as Alfredo and the black van sailed through the red light at Sheridan Road. A taxi with a man and a woman in the backseat was passing through that same intersection on the green light. Alfredo hit them dead center. The car doors burst open as the taxi spun around like a lurching drunk, spilling the occupants onto the street.

Alfredo exited the van through the windshield. He remained alive for the seven-tenths of a second it took to fly into the mailbox on the corner, crush his skull and break his neck. Years later, Lupe would drink Cuban rum with her boyfriend Enrique and joke: "That son-of-a-bitch died going air mail."

The couple, who had been in the back of the taxi, skidded and flailed along the pavement like two rag dolls, entwined with each other until they rolled to a stop against a parked car. The man's eyes were open but unseeing.

The woman's eyes fluttered open and she moaned from low in her belly. Shock kept her from feeling any pain at the moment, but she screamed when she ran her hand over her face and she felt the sticky blood cover her fingers.

The driver of the taxi had it the easiest. Never a healthy man, he died when the little bulge in a blood vessel in his brain popped. Blood like a faucet pumped into his skull, first graying his vision, then blacking it out forever.

Juliana looked out the window of the taxi and shook her head. "Why couldn't you just get a grilled cheese sandwich at the hotel?"

"Because I hate eating in hotels," said Rod. "The service stinks and I hate paying tourist rates."

"So now we drive around with," she leaned forward to look at the driver's tag on the back of the seat "Hameed, looking for the elusive grilled cheese sandwich. How much do you think the cab fare is going to add to the cost of your lunch?"

"I really don't care at this point," he said. But of course he realized she was making perfect sense; he just didn't want to admit he was being childish.

She leaned forward in the seat and said to the driver, "Hameed? Where is the best grilled cheese sandwich in all of Tulsa?"

Hameed, who was used to being asked the whereabouts of drugs and hookers, looked suspiciously in the rearview mirror, unsure whether or not he was being made fun of.

"Grilled cheese? What is grilled cheese?"

"See," she said to Rod. "Even Hameed, the finest taxi driver in Tulsa, doesn't know where to get a decent grilled cheese sandwich. Hameed, is there a Denny's Restaurant near here?" she asked.

"Yes, yes! Denny's! I take you there." He seemed disappointed that the couple finally had a destination in mind. "Ten minutes, no more," he said.

Juliana leaned back with a look of satisfaction. Without turning her head, she said to Rod between her teeth, "This better be the best goddamn G-C-S you ever had."

And Rod, who occasionally knew when to shut up, did. They drove for a few minutes on I-244 and then exited at Sheridan Road.

Hameed, who had gained all his driving skills in Beirut, timed the next green light and accelerated through it, trusting to Allah that no stragglers would go through. He was wrong. A rusty black van came barreling through the intersection almost twice as fast as his cab, hitting him dead center on the right side.

Juliana had been looking out her window. She turned her head and looked out Rod's window on her right, half a breath before the van hit them.

The initial blow crushed them together, snapping Rod's left arm where Juliana's elbow had come up in defense. As the taxi spun around, Rod's door flew open and they were thrown out into the street.

Although he had been taught all the techniques at the Academy, Agent Jackson never liked following people in cars. It just wasn't as easy as it looked in the movies. He especially didn't like it when he wasn't the one driving, because civilians got way too excited and took too many chances. Nonetheless, he was riding shotgun with a taxi driver who, when asked if he could follow another taxi replied: "Yes! I watch French Connection many times!"

"Terrific," said Jackson. "Just don't get too close and don't let them get too far away, either, okay?"

"Okeydokey," said the driver, displaying a magnificent set of white teeth above his black beard. Then he lowered his voice and asked, "Are you going to shoot them?"

Jackson looked at the driver conspiratorially, winked, and said, "Only if I have to. Now let's get going."

Jackson thought he had never seen another human being as happy as his driver looked right at that moment. The guy actually did a fairly good job of following the other taxi, staying about a quarter of a block behind and managing to keep it in sight. They got on a highway for about five minutes and then got off at the Sheridan Road exit. He saw the other taxi speed up to make a green light, and then watched in horror as the black van blew the red and plowed straight into his marks.

Chapter Nineteen

CLOSE QUARTERS

Mike Balcom-Vetillo

Oklahoma

In the dim light of the closet, Brad squinted to check his watch. For a moment he wondered if he had entered the wrong apartment. Too much time had passed. Could someone have entered without him hearing? Had Alice and Jim stopped along the way? He needed to stretch his legs and relieve the tension. It would be easy to open the door, take a quick walk around the room and start the circulation again. Then he could re-position himself and return to the waiting.

Certain he had time, he straightened and began opening the closet door. At the same moment, a key clicked in the apartment's lock. He froze. The discomfort in his legs disappeared. No one spoke. He heard two sets of steps back and forth across the threshold and what sounded like baggage pulled across the floor. Then came the sound of a man grunting and a woman's amused laugh.

"I've lifted grenade launchers that weigh less!" It was Jim.

Alone, the plan had seemed simple enough. Once the closet door opened he would grab the person, put a gun to their head and ... And what? Brad's neck muscles tightened, hearing Jim's husky voice. This wouldn't be easy.

He heard the familiar snap of a refrigerator door opening. "Not much here, Alice. You on some kind of diet or something?"

Her soft laugh, her familiarity, created momentary doubt in Brad's mind.

"Things spoil," she said. "We should have stopped. Isn't there a beer or two in there?"

"Not in this refrigerator."

Again Brad heard soft laughter from Alice. "Let me look." Her footsteps crossed the apartment followed by the sound of items shuffling on metal shelves.

Jim laughed. "But I was looking for a brown bottle," he said, his tone defensive.

The room became quiet. Brad wondered if he had made a noise. Were they sneaking up on him? He readied his gun, wishing he had set the hammer back before they arrived. Now he'd lose a valuable half second.

"Mmmm. Nice, Jim."

They were kissing? Jim began to say something but his voice became buried in the roar of an airplane flying directly overhead. Brad felt the closet shake.

Jim's shout overlapped the roar. "God, Alice, could you live any closer? How can you sleep?"

"It's comforting," she answered. "And it's a short drive. I've walked to the airport."

There came more shuffling and baggage moving. He heard a zipper. "These need to be hung up. I don't want them wrinkled."

Brad gripped the gun tighter.

"Let me help you," Jim said.

Both of them at once, he thought.

"I can manage," Alice teased, and then continued, "You need your rest after all that luggage."

"That's your call," Jim answered, followed by a whoosh, as if he fell back into a cushioned chair.

Then Brad heard footsteps approaching the closet. He suddenly felt exposed. He would be standing directly in her sight the moment the door opened. She would scream and run away. He crouched to the side. The door opened. Alice's arm reached for a coat hanger and he grabbed her wrist.

She screamed and yanked with all her strength, forcing Brad to lose his balance. He fell on her pinning her to the floor. Sensing that Jim would enter the room any second, he grabbed Alice by the throat and pushed the gun against her head. "Stand up and shut up."

Jim charged into the bedroom, his expression shocked as he tried to comprehend the situation. "What the fuck!"

Brad answered by pressing the gun harder against Alice's head. "Do it!"

Jim froze. Brad shouted. "Stand next to her. Face the wall!" He had control now. The decisions were his. He stared at their backs, pulled out his cell phone, and dialed Juliana's number.

Juliana tried to remember what had happened. There was the time she had tried to hit her brother with a baseball bat but missed. Her swing had so much force that she lost her balance, fell and hit her head on the concrete knocking herself unconscious. Then, in high school, she had fought with the football team's quarterback when he wanted to break up with her. She threw him to the ground. He only hit her when she began to bite through the skin on his arm. He didn't intend it, but the force of his punch gave her a mild concussion. And there were all of the bar fights, the nights of wild drinking, the drugs.

Which moment in time is this, she wondered, awareness creeping back. Where am I? There were no links to reality, nothing to grab hold. Am I in high school? In a bar? What happened?

Only a pinpoint of daylight entered her eyes. It appeared miles in the distance as if it were an approaching train.

Am I on drugs? She felt zings of pain crisscross her face as she squinted. She reached up to touch her head and felt bandages. There was a light through a small slit in the gauze over her right eye. An attempt to open her left eye brought pain. I'm in a hospital.

The shadow of a person crossed her vision.

"Are you awake? I'm your doctor. Can you hear me okay?"

Juliana nodded. "Hurts."

"We can give you something for that. Can you move your legs for me?"

Panic raced through her thoughts. Are my legs broken? Is my spine damaged? She wiggled her toes.

"Good. Everything seems to be working."

She tried to remember. "What happened?"

The doctor hesitated. "You were in a car accident. You're lucky to be alive." He paused. "I'm sorry to tell you this, but the man you were traveling with is dead."

She suddenly remembered everything. Good riddance, she thought, thinking of Rod, but had the sense to wait a moment before speaking. "My face? What happened to my face?"

"Did you hear what I said? Your companion didn't make it."

"Yes, but my face?"

"We had to stitch your forehead. It took eighty stitches and there's a deep gash on your cheek that took another fifty. You'll need cosmetic surgery. For now we want you to rest. I'll get you something for the pain."

"How long do I have to stay here?"

"We want to observe you at least overnight. Is there someone you want us to call?"

"No. I'll be okay. Where are my things?"

He pointed. "The closet."

He left the room. She gritted her teeth before forcing her left eye open. A moment later a nurse entered with the pain pills. Juliana pretended to take them. "Thanks," she said, wiping her mouth as the nurse left.

Alone in the room, she carefully eased out of the bed and shuffled to the bathroom. Looking at herself in the mirror she saw hints of blood and antiseptic darkening a long strip on the bandage. She touched one spot and felt swollen numbness through her cheek. "Damn you, Rod!" Composing herself, she found her purse in the closet, and pulled out her cell phone. A small envelope indicated she had one message. After dialing her number the words BRAD'S IN appeared.

She dressed and slipped out of the hospital.

Before facing the wall, Jim noticed red marks on Alice's neck. He glanced into her eyes and saw confidence. He knew he could count on her to back him or to lead the way whatever happened. His first thought was to turn and rush Brad. He'd get shot, but Alice would be safe. No, he would wait until the right distraction came. He turned his head toward Brad. "If you hurt Alice, I'll kill you. You know that, don't you? I'll kill you."

"Face the wall!"

Jim detected hesitancy in Brad's voice. "You gonna tell us what's going on?"

Brad remained silent. Jim laughed, and then asked in an offended voice, "Is it something I said?" He glanced toward Alice, wanting an indication she appreciated his humor. She smiled but then raised both eyebrows, her eyes narrowing. Jim wondered if that meant she thought he was being foolish. He persisted. "Goddamn, Brad, give us a clue. What's going on? Something I did? Something Alice did? Maybe you've got the wrong facts. This could be a mistake."

"No mistake," he answered. "Your wife can explain when she gets here."

"Juliana?" Jim hit the wall with a fist. "You're in with her? Damn! I thought you were smarter than that, Brad."

"Smart? You're the dummy with millions in the bank collecting dust."

"Millions? She told you I have millions?"

"Don't bullshit me, Jim. I know all about the inheritance and the insurance. Maybe you're too stupid to know how much money you actually have."

Another plane flew over. The apartment shook with noise. "Okay, if I have millions, why do you need Juliana? Go ahead and take it all. I don't care."

"It's her money, too. Don't forget you're married. With you dead, Juliana gets it all."

"You trust her? She'll turn on you, too."

"After two years I think I know her."

Jim thought a moment. "Two years? Since the plane crash? Then ... You son of a bitch!"

Jim turned away from the wall and charged at the same time the roar of a passing plane shook the apartment. Brad pulled the trigger. The bullet slammed into Jim's shoulder, knocking him back onto the floor. As he fell he shouted: "You killed my parents!" He lay still for a moment, then attempted to get up, but Alice turned away from the wall and held him back.

"He'll kill you!"

Brad pointed the gun. "She's right. I'll kill you."

Jim didn't stop, pushed at Alice and tried to stand. "You're gonna kill me anyway," he said as he struggled to one knee. Before he could regain his balance, Brad hit the side of his head with the gun. Jim again fell back.

"You'll die when I say so." Brad pulled off the bedspread and threw it toward Alice. "Stick this on his shoulder. I don't want blood all over the place." He watched her bunch up a corner and press down on the wound. "You've got me wrong, Jim. I don't want to kill nobody. Never did. Your wife's the vicious one. I just give her advice. That's all. Advice. She brought the plane down."

Alice helped Jim sit up on the floor against the side of the bed. She put her arm around him. Brad laughed. "You cheating on your wife, Jim? Go ahead and get cozy. We'll just wait until she gets here."

Alice rotated the bedspread as each new section became saturated with blood. Jim had seen gunshot wounds in Vietnam. He touched Alice's hand and whispered, "It's not as bad as it looks."

Someone knocked on the door. Brad motioned them to be quiet and moved closer to Alice, forcing the gun against her head.

"Ask who it is," he whispered.

She cleared her throat. "Who's there?"

"Jackson. You guys decent?"

Alice looked at Brad. His gaze skipped from Jim to Alice to the door. He stepped closer to Jim. "You say anything, anything at all, and she's dead."

Jim nodded. Brad motioned Alice toward the door. He stepped aside as she turned the knob and pulled it open.

Jackson immediately reached out and stepped in to hug Alice. "Girlfriend! Aren't you a sight for . . ."

Before he could say more, Brad pushed the door. Alice screamed. Before Jackson could react, Brad again pressed the gun up against Alice's head. "Do as I say."

"I won't do anything, Brad," Jackson assured him, composing himself. "Stay calm. Tell me what to do."

"Start by facing the wall. Now! Do you have a gun? A knife? Give them to me."

Jackson reached down toward his ankle.

"Stop!" Brad yelled. "I'll kill Alice, I swear I will if you try anything."

"I won't, Brad." Jackson reached in and slowly pulled a chromed-plated gun from his shoulder holster. "I'll pull it out with two fingers, then I'll set it on the floor. Okay?"

Brad agreed. As soon as the gun was on the floor, he picked it up. "Anything more?" he asked.

"That's all."

Brad pulled the hammer back on his gun until it clicked. "No games, Jackson. Otherwise she's dead. Anything more?"

"I swear that's all."

Brad pointed his gun toward the bedroom. "Move! Both of you."

Alice entered first. When she stepped aside, Jackson saw Jim on the floor surrounded by the blood-soaked bedspread. "My God, Jim." Jackson knelt beside him. He checked the wound and turned to face Brad. "He needs a doctor or he's going to die."

Brad smiled. "That's the idea."

He moved toward Brad. "You son of a bitch."

"Easy, Jackson. It's not me. It's his wife. She's pulling the strings here."

"Juliana?" Jackson asked.

"The one and only Mrs. Jim Brill."

Jackson stood. "She's dead, Brad. I saw the accident on the way here. She and Rod were in a taxi. It was broadsided by a van."

"Nice try, asshole."

"Believe me, Brad. She's not coming. It's over."

"She'll be here and we'll walk out of here rich. By tonight you'll all be buried under the new runway."

"How long are you going to wait? You haven't killed anyone. It's all on Juliana so far. Let's get Jim to the hospital. If he dies, it's murder one for you."

Brad shifted his weight from one foot to the other. "She'll be here."

"Listen to me, Brad. I'm with the FBI. I've been following you since the plane crash. We thought you were behind it. Let Jim go to the hospital. I'll tell them you cooperated. Let Juliana be the only murderer."

"Shut up! She'll be here."

"Jim's not going to last long," said Jackson.

"I said shut up!"

Alice sat down on the edge of the bed next to Jim. She looked at Jackson for some assurance. Jackson smiled weakly and nodded.

Jim pressed the bedspread onto his wound. Beads of sweat formed on his brow. He looked up at Jackson. "So you're FBI! Fooled me. I thought you were barely hanging on to your job at O'Hare."

"I said shut up!" Brad shouted again, sweat forming on his brow too.

Someone knocked softly on the door. Brad pulled Alice to him and held the gun to her head before looking out the peep hole.

"Juliana!" He opened the door. She stood there, bandages oozing blood, one eye swollen shut. Brad looked at her, shocked. "What happened?"

Instead of answering she swung out at Alice, knocking her back. "You bitch! You're the first to go." Juliana pulled the gun from Brad's hand and pushed it into Alice's chest. "Say goodbye."

At the same moment, Jackson rushed from the bedroom. Brad saw him and reached down for the other gun. As he raised it to shoot, Jackson grabbed his arm. Brad fought back as he pulled the trigger and shot himself in the leg. He stumbled forward into Alice, pushing her away just as Juliana pulled the trigger. Her bullet slammed into Brad's chest, ripping through his heart. He dropped the gun as he crumpled to the floor.

Juliana froze with the blast, confused with her misfire as Jackson pulled Alice to the floor. In a second he grabbed the gun near Brad's pooling blood, and leveled it at Juliana. "Put it down," Jackson shouted, but she turned and ran.

Chapter Twenty
GUNSHOTS AND WHISPERS
Nancy Wedemeyer

Oklahoma

Jackson took a deep breath of cold air and snapped his head from side to side as he ran out of the building's front door looking for Juliana. He had spent crucial seconds giving directions to Alice about backup and could only guess which way Juliana ran—to the airport, the closest way out of town. He checked the handgun, the number of bullets left in the magazine. Running north, he turned left at the first corner and spotted her a block ahead crossing the street. She was headed for a gap in the airport's perimeter fencing. The injury to her leg caused an unequal gait, a listing to the right like a damaged ship, as she wove back and forth, vision impaired by bandages. Still, she was running fast.

Jackson held the handgun down at his side and dodged a group of children standing on the sidewalk, staring at the back of the fleeing woman. In the backyard of a corner house, people gathered for a picnic looked up, startled, as he ran past. The sound of his labored breathing competed with his thoughts. "If you only knew," he muttered.

As she ducked her head between the chain link sections, wriggling her body sideways, Juliana saw Jackson running full force toward her. She wrenched the snagged sleeve of her blouse from the fence, slicing her upper arm on a jagged wire. Gripping the arm with her gun hand, she took off limp-running faster than before. The whine of planes, in varying stages of take off and landing, pierced the air. Juliana sprinted toward the open bay of a metal hanger visible behind the approaching DC-10. The loosened bandage on her head whipped in the wind like a bloody flag.

"Stop!"

She didn't.

Sirens wailed and Jackson hoped one was the ambulance carrying Jim and Alice to safety. He could imagine Alice's voice on the phone urging emergency services to hurry.

He squeezed through the fence opening and cursed when he heard fabric tear and felt the jab of pain. The same wire that stabbed Juliana gouged Jackson's forearm.

Sparks flew as the bullet struck the fence high and right of his head. The bitch had missed.

Running fast, Juliana twisted back toward the hanger. Jackson, crouching low, used his torn sleeve to wipe the sweat out of his eyes, then raised his gun and lowered it again. Out of range.

The plane's nearness didn't deter Juliana, and Jackson watched her lurch toward it. What was that lunatic thinking, playing chicken with a powerful hunk of metal?

Uniformed guards in the distance waved frantically and shouted warnings, but their words were lost to the air. Jackson saw the pilot gesturing them away as he braked and turned the plane. Security cars raced toward them, sirens screeching and lights flashing.

He was gaining ground, and Juliana was in range, but he couldn't risk a shot; the rescue vehicles were closing fast. "Stop ... Juliana ... Don't . . ."

Juliana kept running as he lunged forward and grabbed her blouse. She stumbled, recovered, tore herself away with a spinning kick that landed on Jackson's chest. She watched as his body skewed sideways, revolver hand swinging over his head. She leveled her gun and fired off a round before Jackson could regain his balance and he collapsed to the ground, left arm hanging limp at his side. The second shot hit the tarmac beyond his head. He raised his arm and fired at the center of her chest as she was caught up in the engine's powerful force. Her feet lifted from the ground, eyes wide with surprise, mouth screaming hate.

He watched from the ground as Juliana disappeared into the engine with a bloody spray. The bird-like shadow of the plane's wing crossed over him like a solar eclipse. He lay on the runway. From somewhere he heard Alice's voice whisper, "Don't die Mr. Opal. Don't die."

Alice paced the surgical waiting room anxious to hear news of Jim. And Jackson. Where was Jackson? Was he all right? Did he catch Juliana? "Oh, God, don't let them die," she prayed. Others in the room slumped in the hard chairs and sipped coffee from paper cups, eyes glazed from uncertainty and lack of sleep.

Remembering Jim's few belongings, his clothes, and especially the copy of Blake, Alice headed for the emergency room to retrieve them. A receptionist, intent on thwarting Alice's plans, stopped her at the doors to the ER and Alice explained her request through clenched teeth.

The outside doors suddenly and quietly slid open admitting a gurney wheeled by paramedics. Three people in scrubs hurried out from the Emergency Room and surrounded the carrier, but not before Alice saw the face behind the oxygen mask. She'd know that face anywhere—had known it since they were children.

"Opal. Jackson. Oh, God," shoving her way to the gurney.

"Stay out of the way," yelled one of the nurses. "Do you know this man? What's his name?"

"Opal. Call him Opal." Jackson's eyelids fluttered with recognition of Alice's voice before she was pushed aside and they rolled the gurney into trauma-room one. The paramedics stopped and turned back to Alice.

"Follow us. Check in with the clerk."

"Where's he hurt? Has he been shot? Tell me something," she shouted.

"Check in with the clerk. They'll get back to you."

Alice hurried instead to the trauma room door and looked through the small square window set at eye level. A team of people began their work. A short, heavyset woman with red hair called out orders. They shifted Jackson side to side, assessing his damage. Someone standing at his head thrust a large instrument like a shoehorn down Jackson's throat and inserted a tube into that before removing the shoehorn. Someone else started an IV and a third person worked on his side. Alice couldn't see what he was doing. These people were blurs of green and blue as they shifted around the table inserting, fixing, patching, assessing, trying to save the life of someone they had never met, while Jackson's best friend stood helplessly by.

The trauma room door opened and two attendants wheeled Jackson to the elevator.

Alice ran to Jackson's side. "Where are you taking him?"

"Surgery."

"What now?"

"Wait."

"Wait. That's all you ever say here."

The red-haired doctor walking behind the gurney stopped, waved the others on and turned to Alice. "I'm Dr. Martin. Can I help you?"

"He's my best friend. Will he live?"

"It's serious—gunshot wound, collapsed lung, and his spleen needs to come out. But he's young, strong—got a good chance. He's FBI?"

"Their best."

Dr. Martin caught the next elevator. Alice turned to go, then remembered the Blake and approached the clerk. She climbed the two flights up to the waiting room again, to wait for news of the two men she loved.

Alice lurched out of her chair when she felt a hand on her shoulder. She had been dreaming about fires and birds flying through the flames while she watched from the ground. She was instantly awake and stared at a man dressed in a green surgical uniform, mask dangling below his chin.

"Here for Jim Brill?"

"How is he?"

"He's in Intensive Care Unit on the third floor. The doctor will talk to you later."

"What about Opal? Jackson Opal?"

"Surgery? I'll find out."

He walked to the desk, made a call and returned within a couple minutes.

"Mr. Opal is in recovery and should be on his way to the same ICU in a little while."

"Yes, but how is he?"

"I'm sorry. I don't have any more information."

The waiting room clerk frowned and shook her head as Alice ran to the elevators.

"Come on, come on," she pleaded with the lighted wall numbers. Kicking the reluctant doors, she turned and ran up the three flights and sprinted down the hallway following the arrows. She checked in with yet another clerk.

"Are you family?"

"Friend."

"I'm sorry, only family members are allowed in Intensive Care." She didn't look sorry. Alice wondered why she kept hearing those two words and hoped it wasn't an omen.

"He doesn't have any family. I'm it."

"Let me check with the nurses."

After a seemingly endless wait, the clerk returned and gave her five minutes.

Jim was connected to every tube and piece of equipment Alice thought she'd seen once in a television hospital drama. His gray face held closed eyes surrounded by puffy, yellow skin. She took a deep breath, hesitated, then approached the bed.

"Jim?" His eyelids opened and closed. Alice picked up his hand. "Jim, it's Alice. I'm here and you're going to be okay." He squeezed her hand and grunted two words that sounded like Alice and Blake. A good sign she thought.

Dr. Martin walked up carrying a chart in a metal holder. She did a double take on Alice's face with a puzzled look on her own. "Aren't you with the wrong patient? Mr. Opal is on his way here now."

"This is another friend."

"Forgive me for asking, but have all of your friends been shot?"

"It's the same situation."

"Ah. Well, we expect Mr. Brill to recover. He'll have some residual ... here's Mr. Opal now," as two men wheeled Jackson's gurney into the glassed-in cubicle next to Jim.

Alice watched as Jackson was transferred to a bed and watched the nurses attach even more equipment to him. Dr. Martin read the monitors and quietly exchanged information with one of the nurses before addressing Alice. "Can you reach Mr. Opal's relatives?"

"Is he going to die?

"Recovery will be long."

"I'm all he has, all they both have."

"A big responsibility."

"They're all I have, too." She walked to Jackson's bed and whispered his name. No response. She spoke a little louder. "Jackson? Opal?"

The tube in his throat prevented speech, but Jackson struggled to open his eyes; Slowly the right lid went up and down. Alice stared. Again the lid opened and closed. He was winking at her.

EPILOGUE

California, six months later

The sun set as golden reflections danced on the waves of the Pacific. "Quite a day," Jim said as he drove up the hill. He was thinking of the small ceremony they participated in a few hours earlier—Peter releasing Charles's ashes on his final earthly flight, the wind carrying their friend gently over the ocean. And how touched he and Alice were that Kirk had delayed this event for six months waiting for Jim to recover from his injuries.

"Yes, quite a day," Alice said, reaching over to change the radio station. She couldn't help noticing how her ring sparkled. Not a typical choice, an opal with diamond baguettes, but just right for her. She leaned over and kissed Jim on the cheek. "Can't wait to get back to the motel."

"Me too."

She paused a moment and asked, "Kirk didn't say why he wanted us to come back to Heaven's Rock?"

"No, but it sounded urgent."

They saw three cars in the parking lot as they crunched to a stop on the white gravel—Kirk's old blue van, and two white rental cars. Flickers of soft candlelight showed dimly through a stained glass window hanging from a beam above one of the patios. As they stepped from the car, they heard Kirk's friendly laughter coming from the church. When they entered, they saw Kirk and Dan sitting across from each other at a small table playing chess by candlelight.

"Gotcha," Dan said, laughing and removing one of Kirk's knights.

"Well, I'll be," Kirk said. "You did it again."

They turned their heads to the front archway.

"Hey, it's about time," Kirk said to Alice and Jim. "Thought you'd never get here." Kirk and Dan rose as Alice and Jim came forward to greet them.

"Dan, what are you doing here? Thought you'd already left for the airport." Alice asked as she hugged him.

"Sit down for a minute," Kirk said, indicating one of the pews, "We'll explain."

Jim and Alice eased down on one of the benches.

Dan sat down at the chess table and leaned back in his chair. "What's going on with you two? You got a ring. When're you getting married?"

Alice and Jim looked at each other. Jim spoke first. "Been a little preoccupied, you know. Gunshot wound. Physical therapy. Moved to Tulsa. Gave all my parents' money to Vietnam vets charities. FBI stuff. No time to register at Wal-Mart."

Alice's glance drifted up to the domed ceiling. Her eyes found the buffalo.

"You know," Kirk said, "it might come as a surprise to you, but as Pastor of this little church, I not only perform funeral services, I perform weddings, too. All perfectly legal, you understand." He stood up and removed the wire-framed reading glasses from his shirt pocket. He put them on and reached for the prayer book resting on the altar. "Here's the deal. A sunset wedding in California and a weekend at our local B and B, compliments of your friends."

Jim's mouth parted. He looked at Alice and back to Kirk. "Hold on. Wait a minute. We don't have a license."

Kirk bent down and shifted Alice's purse to one side, revealing the legal papers. "I have friends in high places," he said, and flipped open the prayer book.

Jim turned to Alice and said softly, "Well, Alice?"

"I only wish . . ." Her thought was interrupted, but her wish came true. There was a rustling at the back of the church.

They all looked up and there stood Jackson Opal, dressed in a dark suit and tie, holding a garment bag. He lifted the bag and strode toward them. "Hi, kids," he said, smiling broadly. "I have a lovely Nordstrom's frock in here. So what's it gonna be, maid of honor or best man?"

THE END

To find out more about the authors of the St. Charles Writers Group, please check the members' website: *http://members.aol.com/stcwritersgroup*